SHE WAS LIKE THAT

Center Point
Large Print

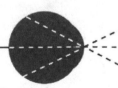

**This Large Print Book carries the
Seal of Approval of N.A.V.H.**

SHE WAS LIKE THAT

NEW & SELECTED STORIES

KATE WALBERT

CENTER POINT LARGE PRINT
THORNDIKE, MAINE

This Center Point Large Print edition
is published in the year 2019 by arrangement with
Scribner, a division of Simon & Schuster, Inc.

The text of this Large Print edition is unabridged.
In other aspects, this book may vary
from the original edition.
Printed in the United States of America
on permanent paper.
Set in 16-point Times New Roman type.

ISBN: 978-1-64358-387-7

The Library of Congress has cataloged this record
under Library of Congress Control Number: 2019946704

SHE WAS LIKE THAT

for my family,
and for Carolyn Cooke

STORIES

M&M WORLD

Ginny had promised to take the girls to M&M World, that ridiculous place in Times Square they had passed too often in a taxi, Maggie scooting to press her face to the glass to watch the giant smiling M&M scale the Empire State Building on the electronic billboard and wave from the spire, its color dissolving yellow, then blue, then red, then yellow again. She had promised. "Promised," Olivia said, her face twisted into the expression she reserved for moments of betrayal. "Please," Olivia whined. "You said 'spring.' "

She *had* said "spring." This she remembered, and it was spring, or almost. Spring enough. Spring advancing, the trees newly budded, the air peppery. Regardless, it felt too early to go home when the light shone this strongly, slanting across Central Park in the way of late March, early April; plus, the city had already collectively sprung forward. *Spring has sprung, the grass has ris'.*

"All right," she found herself saying. "Just once. Today. Just once. This is it." Breaking her resolution to stop qualifying—five more minutes, this last page, one more bite—and wishing, mid-speech, she would stop. She has tried. Just as she has tried to be more easygoing, but when push

13

comes to shove, as it always will, she is not easygoing. And she qualifies. It's a verbal tic: first this and then that. A constant negotiation— action then reward, or promise of reward. What is it that the books say? Screw the books.

She takes the girls' hands and holds tight, changing course, crossing Central Park West to Central Park South. The girls suddenly delighted, and delightful, straining ahead, buoyant. They are gorgeous, bright-eyed, brilliant girls: one tall, one short, pant legs dragging, torn leggings, sneakers that glow in the dark or light up with each step, *boom boom boom*. They break free and race across, bounding onto the sidewalk, their hands rejoined like paper cutouts, zigzagging here, zigzagging there, Maggie clutching Zoom Zoom with her free hand, choking the thing, its dangly legs and arms, its floppy, flattened ears.

Ginny follows them quickly, remembering how her heart would literally stop as Olivia—then what? four? five?—would run to this same corner, the light not yet changed. Her daughter had only to step into traffic, to veer off the curb. She never did. Olivia climbed the stone seals at seal park in Chelsea, the bronze bears in the playground outside the Metropolitan Museum; she teetered on their heads and could so easily have slipped— she did slip, once, but it was nothing. Still, Ginny had to wake her every hour that night, shake her out of her sleepy fog. "Who am I?" Ginny had

14

said, Olivia's blue princess pajamas silky beneath her grip, Olivia's shoulders so thin. "Mommy?" Olivia said, squinting, pupils the right size, shrinking: constricting or contracting, she never knew which, but, whatever, correctly—she was fine. And then, a bit older, those other sneakers—wheelies? heelies?—and Olivia careering along the sidewalk, wheels where the heels should be, the speed! And downhill, too, with nothing to hold on to, no way to stop. The pediatrician had said the most dangerous thing was trampolines, even with nets. And then the rented house that summer had one, netless, in the backyard. She had watched as the girls bounced higher and higher. She couldn't get them off, Olivia and now Maggie, just like her big sister. She had stood vigil at the window, or next to the rail in her hat and long sleeves buttoned at the wrist, the girls slathered with sunscreen. The point is, her heart stuck in her throat, always in her throat.

Ginny hurries to catch up. One has tripped the other accidentally on purpose and now the other howls as if singed with fire.

"Stop it," Ginny hisses. "Right now. Period. Stop it or no M&M World."

They stop, Olivia smiling to clear the air, though the air stinks: they're near a line of carriages and their horses.

"Please," Maggie's saying. "Please. Please." And so they circle around, petting Blackie,

15

petting Whitey, petting Gummie with the drippy nostrils, the one the driver says loves sugar— "Yes, yes, next time we'll bring a sugar cube"— and Whinny and Happy and the other one, its long yellow teeth reminding her: she needs to bleach. Suddenly everyone's teeth are whiter than her own; they wear them like necklaces. And their faces, too, seem suspiciously doctored, first one line then another magically evaporating, a whole generation of women paying for erasure.

"Ouch," Maggie says. She holds one hand flat as instructed, the brown carrot there, a gift from the driver. The driver laughs. "No danger," he says. The horse roots and chews. "You're fine," Ginny says. She strokes the soft hair of the horse's muzzle, the horse nuzzling Maggie's tiny palm; it wears a hat with a feathered plume, as if it had trotted here from the stables of a fallen tsar. Ginny leans into its solid skull, and the horse stares back at her with a huge watery eye. Where am I? it wonders, or something equivalent, and she thinks of the whale in Patagonia that asked the same thing. This was years ago, before the girls were born, when she and the girls' father took a trip to Chile.

They were there for vacation; there to see animals. Animals had been promised, including whales. A center existed, manned by earnest students, young men and women from all over the world who spoke Spanish beautifully and wore thin silver bracelets with a symbol that meant something. They piloted the boats and explained to the tourists the seriousness of the venture, the need for extra donations. The tourists kept quiet, mostly, standing on the side of the boat where they'd been told to stand, given the radar and various other instruments that would determine the location of the whales— sometimes a female with a calf or two or, rarer, a male on its own. The whales communicated over great distances, as everyone knew, but the students could intercept their communications, or decipher them: regardless, somehow the students knew what the whales were saying, or might be saying, and so could steer the boat in the right direction, where, for a fee, the tourists could take pictures of the whale surfacing or of the plume of water from the blowhole, or sometimes, even, if the tourists were very lucky, of a whale jumping gracefully as if showing off.

On this particular voyage, the one Ginny found herself on with the girls' father, Ginny chose to stay on the side of the boat with more shade. She was hot, she told the girls' father. He could call her if anything exciting happened. She had opened her book: *War and Peace*, a paperback edition she had picked up in the paperback exchange in Santiago, where they had stayed for a few days before heading south. She had been at a good part, a really good part, and so perhaps it took some time for the whale to get her attention. She had had, when she later thought about it, the feeling of being watched. And so she had looked up from her place in *War and Peace* and seen the whale, a female, she would learn, uncharacteristically alone, lolling before her on the surface of the water. She folded the corner of her page and stood, shading her eyes; then she walked to the boat rail to get a better look. She didn't call the girls' father; she didn't call anyone. She looked down at the whale. It lay on its side, staring with one eye straight at Ginny, drifting alone in its disappearing sea, the sun burning both of them, beaming through the torn shreds of the shredded atmosphere. They stayed like that for a while, Ginny convinced that the whale had a message to deliver, something she might translate and convey to the world. But she never figured out what, since too soon someone from the other side saw it and the whale was gone.

"Mother!" Maggie's saying.

Ginny pulls away from the solid skull of the horse and turns back to her youngest.

"You weren't listening," Maggie is saying.

"Was so," Ginny says.

"Then can I?" Maggie says.

Ginny bends down to kiss Maggie's head, the part between the plastic barrettes that Maggie repeatedly refastens each morning, wanting to look, she says, "right." Maggie's hair smells delicious.

"No," she says.

Maggie stomps her foot; she's pushed Zoom Zoom deep in her pocket, its strange face, not quite rabbit, not quite anything else—"it's extinct," Maggie once said—just above the fold.

"I love you," Ginny says. "You're beautiful."

"What about me?" Olivia says. She has been standing next to Ginny, as quiet as a stone.

"You, too, sweetheart," she says, pulling her oldest in. "You, too."

There are other things to fix, not just her yellow teeth. She needs some spots removed from her skin; she needs to dye her gray roots, the stubborn tuft that refuses to blend. She could use something for her posture—Pilates—and she's overdue a mammogram, a bone scan, a colonoscopy. She needs a new coat, an elegant one like those she's seen on other mothers, something stylish to go with the other stylish clothes she means to buy, and the boots, the right boots, not just the galoshes she's slipped on every morning all winter; it's spring now, isn't it? She should pay to have her toes soaked, her feet scrubbed of dead skin. She could choose a bright color of nail polish, a hip color, a dark purple or maybe even that shade of brown. She should take a class—philosophy, religion, vegan cooking—and wear sandals there, the new kind, with the straps that wrap the ankle or twist all the way to midcalf, her brown toenails shiny smooth, as if dipped in oil. There are posters on the subway and numbers to call. She writes down the websites in the notebook she carries for such things: lists, reminders. But she is constantly out of time, losing track, forgetting. Sunday's Monday evening, then Wednesday vanishes altogether.

M&M World looms in the distance, the electronic billboard—m&m's world—as bright as a beacon. They hurry down Broadway. At Fifty-first, Olivia claims she can see the waving M&M hanging from the spire of the Empire State Building. "It's blue!" she says.

"Where? Where?" Maggie says.

"No, it's green!" she says.

"Where?" Maggie says, hopping. She's suddenly furious. "I can't see! Lift me!"

"Be patient," Ginny says. She takes Maggie's hand and pulls her along. Olivia is in front, swimming upstream, parting the crowds. Hallelujah to the end of the hideous winter: blackened snowdrifts and dog shit and lost gloves. The city erupts, oozes, overflows; everyone is outdoors, walking quickly or standing on the corner checking phones, dialing phones, speaking on phones. "Where?" someone is saying. "You're breaking up."

"Olivia?" she yells; she doesn't see her.

Olivia has stopped in front of a store window: snow globes and hats and luggage on wheels, a rack of I ♥ New York T-shirts, electronic gadgets. She is suddenly taller when she turns back around, her face complicated. "I'm here, Mom," she says.

"Don't scare me."

"It's the new kind."

"I can't," Ginny says. "We've got to—"

Maggie's pulling her hand. "Mister Softee!" she's saying.

Christ, already? The truck?

"Please?" Maggie says.

"Not today," Ginny says.

"Did you see it?" Olivia's saying.

"Just a minute," she says to Maggie. "What?" she says to Olivia.

"Please? It's a special day, isn't it?" Maggie's saying. "It's spring. You said." Ginny turns to Maggie. In Maggie's smile are four missing teeth, each one saved and wrapped in tinfoil in her Tooth Fairy Box. She plans on blowing her wad all at once: fifteen teeth—or are there more?—beneath her pillow, precious little things although three have already been patched for cavities, the dentist wondering how vigilant Ginny has been about flossing, the amount of candy consumed. "Remarkably so and hardly any," Ginny had said at the last appointment. "It's a mystery."

21

"Next time," she says now to Maggie. "Enough's enough."

"It's the new kind," Olivia is saying.

Maggie looks up. "Please," she says, her teeth tiny pearls.

"Mom!" Olivia says.

"Oh, all right," Ginny says. "Just this once. Not again. Only because it's spring. This is it."

"Thanks, Mom," Maggie says, smiling.

"What?" Olivia says.

"Ice cream!" Maggie says. They high-five and dance around Ginny's knees.

Ginny had kept a list of the animals of Patagonia. The ones that interested her. There were the penguins, of course, an entire colony that was completely tame. They had never been hunted and it was as simple as that, the guide had said, she and the girls' father stooping, squatting to watch them furiously building their nests: the mating season had ended and now they were preparing for eggs. There were some, too, that were not well. Those stood on the outside of the colonies looking in; sometimes small crowds of other penguins gathered around them and nosed them toward the water, a not so subtle suggestion, the guide had said, that they might be better off drowned. Brutal nature, the girls' father had said. There were the lizards and the guanacos and the numerous birds, the elephant seals they'd

22

watched from a cliff top, the males fighting over a female that lay on its side, clueless or, rather, helpless. Brutal nature, she had said, and the girls' father had laughed, and in that instant, and this is true, a rainbow had appeared—it was that kind of weather—the arc stretching from one end of the ocean to the other, and she had taken his hand and said, "Yes." She thought she was ready. Children, she had said. Dozens of them.

There are even more people farther on, in Times Square, though the cars have been blocked and so there's that, at least—one less thing. They'll finish their ice creams here before turning back toward the store, Ginny says, maneuvering the girls around the tables and chairs, the feet, the flocks of pigeons, the remnants of lunches consumed. Men and women she may or may not recognize—movie stars, rappers, models—loom above them, magnified a thousand percent, their eyes the size of swimming pools, their teeth cliff walls she could hide behind or possibly dwell in, like the Anasazi, chiseling toeholds so she might scale down at night to forage. The movie stars, rappers, and models are invariably smiling, cheerful; some sing or dance, the women with suggestive postures, the men in dark glasses and fur coats. Everyone is moving, gyrating, blinking, flashing. Tourists sit on the new risers watching nothing or everything, looking down, from time to time, to study their guidebooks. The breeze picks up, eddying ticket stubs and wrappers and waxed paper and brown bags and plastic straws and whatever else has been left behind. Shameless, this litter: if she ran the world. Recently, a flock of plastic bags has caught in the spindly sycamore in front of their apartment, empty bags that inflate and deflate with the wind like marooned sailing ships. They are what she sees when she looks out the living room window, which, truth be told, she does more often now than she should. It's as if she were trying to remember something that she'd forgotten, as if there were someone she was supposed to call. She stands at the window and looks, the plastic bags inflating, deflating. Alive, somehow, mocking her or maybe just reminding her—a cosmological message. From whom? Of what?

"Mother!" Olivia yells. Maggie, halfway between Ginny and Olivia, is on the pavement, clutching her knee. "Mister Softee!" she's saying. "My cone!" Ginny is next to her before she knows it, pushing up Maggie's ragged leggings to expose the skin, stroking her hair. Strangers gather dumbly. "We're fine," Ginny says. "Thank you. She's fine." She blows on the scraped place, red and scratched raw but not bleeding—they were racing, they were almost tied, Olivia's explaining. Maggie's ice cream is upturned and melting in the street, a ruination. Maggie cannot speak for sobbing. "Sweetheart," Ginny's saying, stroking her hair. "It's okay, sweetheart. We'll find another truck. We'll get a new one. We'll get another."

Olivia licks her cone, listening. "Then I want another one, too," she says.

The place is jammed and loud. There are vats of brightly colored M&M's everywhere, M&M's crammed in plastic tubes spiraling to the ceiling. There are M&M T-shirts and M&M mugs and M&M tote bags and stuffed M&M men, or whatever they're called (M&M guys? M&M characters?), and M&M pillows and M&M beach towels and M&M statues and M&M key rings and M&M snow globes and M&M plates and M&M puzzles and M&M umbrellas. The employees, dressed in M&M colors, dance and sing along—for minimum wage?—to a song Ginny recognizes, a song she's heard played continuously on the radio station that Olivia listens to in her room now, the door mostly closed. It's the voice, Olivia pointed out, of one of the men on the billboards, one of the men swathed in fur—or maybe he was the guy in the suit. Ginny can't remember, her head already clogged, her eyes watering. It is hot in here, the air-conditioning not yet on, the heat remembering winter. The girls stand on either side of her, transfixed. Maggie's tears have been wiped dry, a Band-Aid found in the deep recesses of Ginny's purse, the wound, as Maggie called it, cleaned with a hand wipe, then kissed for good luck. Only Big Sister could do that part—wiggling her fingers first to conjure the fairy dust that only Big Sister could conjure. A fairy dust invisible to mothers, its healing powers a mystery, like phoenix tears, Olivia said. Or Zoom Zoom, Maggie said.

"Can we, please?" Olivia asks now. She has seen the sign directing customers up, by way of the escalator, to the second floor, where a life-size M&M waits like Santa Claus, available for photographs.

"All right," Ginny says. "Just this once. Because we're here. But not if there's a line."

"Yeah!" the girls say. Olivia takes Maggie's hand and leads the way. Ginny watches them step onto the escalator with their identical ponytails, their small shoulders, their fleeces tied around their waists. From the moment they were born, they looked like her or they looked like their father, or, sometimes, they looked like a combination of both: her hair and his eyes, his mouth and her nose, her chin and his smile. But from behind now they look just like little girls: sisters in a portrait, or Renoir's beauties in flat black hats, poppies sprung from their ballet shoes. They are timeless, somehow, though too fast growing. "Zoom Zoom is shrinking," Maggie

26

had said. "Wasn't Zoom Zoom once bigger?" They ascend and Ginny feels the catch of love unbearable: she never imagined this, she thinks, her heart suddenly thudding, as if stepping down a stair or two, hard, and then a pause and then another thump, or a clump, her heart clumping down the stairs—caffeine, maybe, or nerves.

She follows them up but they are already out of sight. The crowds thick, people speaking different languages, laughing, dancing with the employees. Where is she? What is this? At the top of the stairs, Olivia waits to show her. "Look!" she says, holding up a green Statue of Liberty M&M. "You pull the torch."

"Cool," Ginny says.

"Are you looking?" Olivia says. "The torch!"

"I saw," Ginny says. "It's cool."

"And they have purple ones."

"Cool."

"Can we get some?"

"Where's your sister?"

"With the guy. Can we get some?"

"What?"

"The purple ones! They're grape!"

She and the girls' father had discussed at length how to explain it to them. He had thought it best to be as honest as possible, to sit them down and simply tell them that he was moving out. "They're old enough," he had said.

They're too young, she'd said. She could barely look at him. He was all secrets; they slid around beneath his expression like tectonic plates. He was all the things he wouldn't say to her that she wanted to know, all deception and cunning. It made her crazy to look at him and so she stared at her feet, at her ubiquitous galoshes. At least she should find some more contemporary ones, the ones with the thick matching socks turned down over the top, the ones in strong solid colors that came from the British Isles or somewhere—Brittany?—and suggested other lives, lives spent mucking stalls or milking cows, or even striding with a fishing rod and a rough-hewn basket through streams where the trout still ran as they once had, before, in other places, they grew strange scales and forgot to spawn; lives spent striding and oblivious of the wet, oblivious of the hard stones that would have pierced the soles of lesser girls. Boots that suggested strength or, at the very least, a day's catch.

"It's not like they don't get the concept," he had said.

She looked up at his face and squinted, and the girls were there, too: in his eyes, his eyebrows.

"Maggie!" Ginny shouts. She can't see her. The line for a photograph with the M&M is endless, and she can't see Maggie anywhere.

"What guy?" Ginny asks, turning to Olivia. "What do you mean, 'the guy'?"

"I didn't say that," Olivia said. "I don't know. She was here a minute ago."

"Where?"

"Right here," Olivia says, and starts to cry.

"Don't," Ginny says. "We'll find her. Please. She wouldn't just disappear. She's got to be somewhere. Maggie!"

"Maggie!" Olivia says.

"Maggie!" Ginny says.

There are too many people in M&M World. There should be some requirements, some restrictions. She's quite sure that numerous fire codes are being broken. She plans to write a letter, to get someone's attention—she'll call 311. There are hundreds of people, if not thousands, in this place. How can anyone see a thing? She looks around at the racks, the ascending columns of stuff, the stacks and piles beneath the garish lights, and she suddenly thinks she spots Maggie, but it's not her; it's another child. She yanks Olivia here and there. "Maggie!" she calls. She is trying to remain calm. She'll find an employee in a minute; there must be an intercom system. "Maggie!" This must happen all the time, as it does at Disney World and places like that. The store can automatically lock the doors. "Maggie!" She sees an employee, a girl no more than seventeen or eighteen in M&M green with a pierced nose and spiky blond hair. "My daughter," she says, breathless, flagging her. "She's gone." The girl's name tag says WENDY, KALAMAZOO, MICHIGAN. Thank God, a midwesterner.

"I mean, she was with me. And now I don't know where she is."

"Was she here?" Wendy says.

"Yes, she was. With me. And I can't—" Ginny breaks away. "Jesus, is there someone else?"

"I'll help you find her," Wendy says.

"Is there a manager?"

"Don't panic," Wendy says.

"I've got to—"

"Barbara," Wendy is saying into some kind of apparatus she's wearing around her neck.

She and the girls' father sat across from each other at the kitchen table, the light above them harsh, the hour late. From time to time, an ambulance sirened by, or someone shouted in the street; it was the weekend. The girls slept in the other room, Olivia with the quilt wrapping her ankles—she tossed and turned—and Maggie with Zoom Zoom and her other animals positioned around her. Zoom Zoom in the doll cradle, perhaps, or tucked in a towel on the floor, its head on a pincushion or a neatly folded Kleenex.

He talked and talked. She needed a change in subject; she needed to go to bed. It was all

30

so banal, wasn't it? So ordinary? Predictable? An intern? A true love? She looked down at her unvarnished nails: in college she had worn leather moccasins and, on occasion, feathers in her ears; she'd won a prize for her dissertation. Most days, she carried a tote bag, black, with the name of her favorite nonprofit in white.

She listened for a while, and then she did not. Then she said, "Maybe we could tell them it's like what happens when they argue about the fort. How they each want to push the other out of the fort, how there's never enough room in the fort. We could tell them you're taking a break from the fort," she said.

"All right," he said.

"This, of course, makes me the fort," she said.

"You are not the fort," he said.

"I was joking," she said.

Outside, a bottle shattered.

"But they might understand the thing about the fort," she said.

"All right," he said.

"They might," she said.

"That's good," he said.

"Maggie!" Ginny yells. She feels Wendy touch her arm, right behind her.

"Don't leave," Wendy says. "That's the first thing."

"What?"

"Don't go out of sight."

"She's out of sight," Ginny says. "My daughter. She's five years old. Please."

Olivia cries beside her. "I'm sorry," Olivia says. "It's my fault."

"It's not your fault," Ginny says. "Sweetheart, it's not your—Maggie!" Now Ginny's screaming, her voice swallowed by the wall of sound, the same song, the same rapper, repeatedly singing. Customers stop browsing, unsure what to do. They step back and multiply, as if viewing an accident.

Wendy is speaking into the gadget around her neck. She looks up. "Barbara's on her way," she says, as if delivering good news. "She was in inventory."

After the whale swam away—disappeared, really—Ginny couldn't quite explain to the girls' father why she hadn't called him immediately. He had promised to call her, he said, so why hadn't she called him? He had been just on the other side of the boat; he had the camera, after all. He hadn't seen a thing, he said. By the time he heard the other tourists shouting, the hubbub, the whale was gone and Ginny was standing there, red-handed. "You were red-handed," he teased her afterward. "A whale hoarder."

"Was not a whale hoarder," she'd said.

"Uh-huh," he said. "Whale hoarder."

And for a while, in the early years of their marriage, when she spent too much time reading, or rose early to walk alone in the park, or drifted off when the two were having dinner in a restaurant, he'd kick her ankle and say it again. "Whale hoarder," he'd say. And she'd laugh and then she would not. She'd remember the whale's expression, how it lay on its side and drifted in the current, how it had been so close that she could see the raised scars of its skin, the mottled gray color of it and the sheen of evaporating water, and its massive head, how the whale's eye, onyx black, had looked directly at her, unblinking, and she had thought, If I can stand here long enough, if I can just look hard enough, I'll understand. What, she wasn't sure, but she felt it was something she was meant to know, something beyond the noise of everything else, something as clear as the sounds carried across the ocean. "What?" she had said to the whale. "What?"

It is Olivia who spots Zoom Zoom after Barbara has arrived and the doors have been manned, after Ginny has sunk to the floor with her head between her legs, after the tourists, English-speaking and those with no idea, have come forward, rallying around the woman with the missing child and the child that remains, a gorgeous girl, freckled, tall, her hair loosened

33

from its ponytail, her face puffed with tears. It is Olivia who sees Zoom Zoom's ear, and then Maggie's shoes, or the bottoms of them, beneath the dressing room curtains, Maggie covered by a heap of discarded M&M wear, an M&M beach towel over her head. She hadn't heard her mother or her sister, she said, howling. She thought they'd gone, too.

"Too?" Ginny says, hugging her youngest to the floor, hugging her small arms and legs, folding her into her own arms as tight as she can bear. "Too?" she says, crying, laughing, pulling Olivia in as well, so that the three form a kind of solid thing, a weight, a substance, as round as a boulder, which, for the moment, fills in the empty space that was there just before. And suddenly everything returns: the buzzy air, the lemony chocolate scent piped through the store, the rapper's song, the rainbow wall of colors, the crowds.

"Let's go," Ginny whispers. The girls are sniffling, their faces hot. She stands then, a daughter gripped in each hand. They ride the escalator down in silence, staring out the large windows toward Broadway, toward the familiar thickening rush-hour crowd, until they reach the bottom and step off. Ginny lets go first, leading them, pushing hard on the glass door against the wind, against what has become more than a blustery day, because in truth it is not yet spring, exactly; there is still the possibility of a freeze.

She squats to zip the girls' fleeces to their chins, to kiss their cheeks—their eyes still wet with tears—then pulls them close to her, again. How soon the whale dissolved into its darkening sea. How soon she was left on her own, waiting.

THE BLUE HOUR

Today I've been watching it snow and thinking of Katharine. This was in Rochester, before your sister was born, when you were four or five and your father worked most weekends. (I have always thought it ironic that your father made our living as an efficiency expert, a job that required so many hours of overtime.) We lived in a pink-brick Georgian at the end of a cul-de-sac called Country Club Road. Your father had flown out from Detroit to find it and had bought it over one weekend. You were too young to travel at the time so we stayed behind. I remember he called from the Holiday Inn to let me know he had found a house and how, when I asked him to describe it, he said it had an "expansive den."

We moved the following weekend and I suddenly found myself in a pink Georgian in the middle of a Rochester winter. I tried to keep my spirits up. I went around to some of the homes where snowmen had been built, ostensibly looking for playmates for you. Katharine lived in one of those grand cold Tudors with leaded windows and azaleas and box hedges trimmed into spades. Her Christmas decorations were still out—garlands of evergreen wrapped with white lights and a red-ribboned wreath on the front door. I rang the doorbell and Katharine opened the door as if expecting me. I remember thinking how much she looked like Audrey Hepburn.

"You're here."

"Marion Clark," I said, holding out my hand.

"Oh," she said, shaking it. "I'm sorry."

"You thought I was someone else?" I said. She nodded. "Forgive me, it's cold. Come in."

She was a woman who could say *forgive me* without batting an eye.

The inside of her house felt nothing like the outside; it held a sweet thick smell I recognized as incense. There were large pillows scattered around the floor in the living room and plants whose tendrils grew up and over the windows. I accepted her drink offer, though it was two o'clock in the afternoon and, for those years at least, your father and I had a rule about no cocktails before six.

I asked for an old fashioned. It sounded right. She nodded when I said it as if I had passed a secret test; then she led me into the living room. "You are who I was waiting for," she said, ducking out. I sat on the couch. It was draped with a batik fabric that had hundreds of tiny mirrors stitched into it, and I remember how I thought that if light ever got through those heavy webbed-green windows the mirrors would reflect it like so many diamonds, as if the couch were afire.

Katharine returned with an ornate tray and sat down across from me on one of the floor pillows. "So," she said, handing me my drink. "Let me guess. You're new. You're bored. You're looking for playmates for your child but you're really looking for company."

"I suppose you could say that."

"Well, cheers then," she said, lifting her glass. "To playmates."

"Salud," I said, I'm sure wanting to sound continental. I felt paltry in comparison to this creature in black silk. I had worn my usual wool slacks and snow boots. How could I have known?

I sipped my drink. She had made it quite strong, and from the first taste I felt transported.

"So," she said. "Let me tell you what there is to know. First off, I'm Katharine. I don't think I ever said that. Not Kathy or Katie, please, but Katharine. My mother was very particular about this. Anyone who would call me anything but got a talking-to, including teachers and boy-friends. She named me Katharine after Katharine Hepburn, whom I believe goes by Kate. But Mother's lost so there you have it. Second, I live in this monstrous house with a husband, Rick, and twin sons, Richard and Ross. It was not my idea to go with *R*. In fact, I was completely against it, but Rick insisted so what could I do. I had just been through forty-one hours of labor and you might say my mind was a little foggy,

41

and besides, he's from Canada of all places."
Katharine paused and took a sip of her drink.
Behind her, through the thick glass, I saw that it
had begun to snow again, and wondered if she
wasn't cold in nothing more than silk.

"We moved here about seventeen months ago
and the boys think it's great and Rick plays golf
and I am bored out of my mind. Rochester, for
God's sake. Who would have thought I would
end up here? I am the daughter of missionaries.
I grew up everywhere, including Calcutta and
Beijing, and I am the first to tell you that life is
elsewhere. My mother ran away to find it." She
took a deeper sip. "Do you know what I mean?"

"I suppose so," I said. I felt hot in my coat,
but she hadn't offered to take it. I felt as if I
had entered some sort of circus fun house and
Katharine sat before me as the reflection of what
I could become, if I squinted my eyes, if I poured
a drink at two o'clock and burned incense in
Rochester.

"Oh, I'm not saying there's nothing to do here.
There's the club and a good bridge group and
dances every Saturday and around Christmas
they have the Bachelors' Ball, which is really for
all the married folk who go and get blasted to the
hilt and switch husbands and that sort. We'll talk
about that into the next year and the spring and it
will give us something to think about come fall,
again, when we are feeling kind of blowsy and

old and when we unpack the ornaments and find two shattered, again. Too bad you weren't moved in before that; you could have met the gang and added your own rumor to the mill."

I must say it got to a point where I simply watched her mouth move. I could not get past a woman using the word *blowsy* in a sentence and getting away with it. She sounded so grand. She reminded me of a lone exotic fish, the type you might see in one of those overpriced pet stores swimming around and around and around an aquarium, the glass sides of which are nearly opaque from algae let to grow, as if the poor thing has been forgotten.

"Come on," she said at last, draining her drink. "The boys won't be home for an hour and I need to shop. You come. I want help."

I stood. I'm not sure how much time had passed, but I remember thinking that you would be fine, set with a new babysitter. Katharine walked to the hall closet and put on a very full raccoon coat. Then she opened the front door and stepped out. I followed her around to the garage.

"Don't you need the air?" she said, lighting a cigarette. She stood by the garage door and smoked. "Rick doesn't let me do this in the house and who can blame him, the plants and all. Terrible habit, really. My teeth are yellow. But it gives me something to do, don't you think that? If nothing else, this is something to do." We

43

shared the cigarette, then stamped into the garage and got into her car, the make of which I cannot remember. She was not a woman who would take much stock in automobiles, though she did love clothes and had the most elegant wardrobe of anyone I had ever known, before or since. I remember when I got the news that she was dead my second or third thought was of those clothes, of what they would have chosen to put her in for her burial.

We drove into downtown Rochester fast, through yellow lights just changed to red. She had turned on the radio, and I remember how good it felt to have had one drink and to be riding in the front seat of a warm car in the middle of an afternoon with a new friend. She pulled over once we got to the department store—one of those once-grand chains you find in depressed cities. I felt a bit blue, stepping out of the car into the cold to enter such a faded place. We should have pulled up to Bonwit's and left the keys in the car for the valet. But soon the mood shifted; there were aisles of brightly lit things and a makeup counter where a few well-preserved women stood in lab coats and beckoned us closer. I was game but Katharine took my hand.

"Come on," she said and led me to the escalator, one of the old kind with wooden railings. We rode up to the sportswear section on the second floor.

"What are we looking for?" I asked her.

"You'll see," she said and smiled.

She led me past sportswear toward the back of the second floor, through a maze of girdled mannequins and mounds of flesh-colored bras and panties on sale. The nightgowns hung along the rear wall, a rack of silky expensive things I would have normally passed right by. Katharine stood in front of them. "Aren't they divine?" she said.

They were part of some kind of early Easter display—pink and blue and green and yellow silks. "I can't wear yellow, but you," Katharine said, choosing a yellow one from the rack. "You could do it."

She held the yellow nightgown up to me and admired it. I looked back at her, again thinking of her as some kind of mirror in which I stood reflected. "It's lovely," I said.

Katharine smiled again. "But you do like it?" she said. I took the hanger from her and carried the nightgown over to the real mirror. It was difficult to tell whether I liked it or not. I felt foolish. There I stood in the middle of a Rochester winter holding a yellow silk nightgown over my wool coat and wool slacks, sure that if I actually tried it on I would look absurd in my thick socks and pale arms.

"It's lovely, really," I said, carrying it back to Katharine and putting it on the rack. "Perhaps I'll come back for the sales."

Katharine shrugged. "I think it is a wonderful color for you. Not many can wear yellow," she said.

She stood and stared at me for a moment. I attributed the strangeness I felt to the old fashioned.

She invited me in as we pulled into her garage and I accepted. I had so rarely had company in the afternoons in Detroit. Once inside, she offered another drink. There was something of a party about that day—a new friend, a spontaneous shopping trip, two old fashioneds before six. I felt as if the world could indeed open up for me and I could step in.

She brought out the fresh drinks on a new tray. I pulled off my snow boots and this time she offered to take my coat and I said yes. I felt so comfortable, as if I could curl up on the mirrored couch and sleep for years. I tried to explain the day to your father that night but I could not find the right words.

With Katharine, the right words were easy. I told her about our moves, and about you and your birth. I told her how your father and I hoped to have another child soon.

She told me again how the *R* names had been her husband's idea. She told me again that her parents were missionaries and that the white porcelain elephant in the corner had come directly from Burma, before they had shut the gates, and that her mother was a great beauty with blond hair and that everywhere they had gone the people in the villages had been far more interested in looking at her hair than they had been in hearing her preach about God and Jesus.

Then she asked me did I believe in God and Jesus, and at the time I did, so I said yes.

She said there were plenty of churches she could show me, but that she could not go inside. That she had sworn off it like she had sworn off any more children and any more sex with her husband.

It was at that point I said I should go, not because I disliked her using such an unfamiliar word, but rather because I knew that with Katharine I could say much that I might come to regret, that I could speak words that had been, before this, light as balloons drifting through my mind. To speak them would be to give them hcft and weight.

"Goodbye, love," she said at the door, kissing me on both cheeks. "See you tomorrow?"

"Of course," I said.

She held my coat up for me and I put my arms through the sleeves and felt so entirely warm, from her, from this, from the promise of another day, that I walked home slowly through the bitter cold, balancing on the ridged rain gutters that ran on either side of Country Club Road, slipping some on the ice. It was the part of the day I would later come to know as the blue hour. Katharine said she had picked it up somewhere, she thought perhaps Paris. *L'heure bleu.* She said it seemed to her always the best way to describe that time of early evening when the world seemed trapped in melancholy and all its regrets for all its mislaid plans for the day were spelled in the fading clouds.

This is, quite truthfully, how she would phrase things.

Once home, I picked you up and kissed you, and the two of us drove the babysitter back to wherever she had come from. On our return, we stopped for something at the store. Running in, I reached into my coat pocket for my wallet and felt the silk wadded down so deep, I thought for an instant I had never noticed the fine lining of the wool. Then I pulled it out. The yellow nightgown, of course.

You came to despise Rochester winters, could never play outside, or for only a few hours, since I was a nervous mother and didn't want you too long in the cold. You would stand, your nose pressed to the plate-glass door, amphibian-like fingers out and spread wide. You would wish for anyplace else.

But the next afternoon you were still excited by the newness of it, of your room, of places to go. The babysitter arrived particularly buoyant, a fresh-faced high school girl you might have grown into if we had stayed. You led her up the stairs to the place in the hallway where you had set up your Barbie palace, and I called to both of you that I would be gone a few hours, that I was visiting a friend. That day shone with an unfamiliar light; it had stopped snowing the night before, and a sun that seemed as foreign to that city as a locust storm or a tornado had appeared in the morning through pale clouds. The sky looked like a Renaissance painting of a sky, with pinks and blues and mother-of-pearl grays. It hurt to look at it but that we did, Katharine and I. She had met me at the door and led me outside, where she told me to stand, my back to her back, and stare straight up. Her hair smelled of something herbal, and I could feel her shoulder blades against my own. She wanted us to have our coats off, to lean against one another and to look straight up and to close our eyes and imagine spring.

"Think of yourself standing in the middle of a whiteout and suddenly the white is blown away by a giant fan and everything's clear and you can see for miles and miles," she said, and so I tried, but truth be told I have always had a tough time shutting my eyes and seeing myself. All I could do was smell Katharine's hair and feel her shoulders through her sweater; all I could picture was the one tiny button, looped with silk thread, at the nape of her neck.

I visited Katharine every afternoon and every afternoon she met me at the door, glamorous, as if she had slept in her evening clothes. Winter eventually gave way to a wet spring; the trees shook out their new buds and appeared to blossom, collectively, on one particular day in May. It was a few weeks after that that Katharine met me at the door and put her hand over my eyes. I felt a flutter—her heart, though it might have been my own eyelashes against her skin. Her perfume smelled of cinnamon and tea.

"As you know," she said, leading me in. "I grew up elsewhere. We were missionaries. Or my parents were. Then my mother split. My mother dressed as a boy, a young Arab boy, and toured northern Africa on horseback. I just found out she died, in a flood." I had heard this story before, or most of it. What I did not know was the part about Katharine's mother in costume. My understanding was that she had died years before. My initial reaction was then of surprise not at the news of Katharine's mother's death but at the news that during this long winter we had spent in Katharine's living room, Katharine's mother had roamed the world.

"This arrived yesterday," Katharine said, taking her hand away. "Ta-da!"

Before me, raised awkwardly on the Persian rug I had admired many times on the floor of Katharine's living room, was a tent unlike any I had ever seen. It had many peaks, for starters, and from each a small flag hung, limply; the fabric was the color of sand and across its surface were painted hundreds, perhaps a thousand pairs of eyes, each startled, each oddly female.

"It came in the mail. I think she painted it. I don't know. Anyway, it arrived in a box, with her." Katharine lit a cigarette. "She wants me to take her somewhere. To spend the night in this and then to throw her out."

"Her?" I said.

Katharine gestured to a small urn on the coffee table. "Will you come?" she asked.

"Of course," I said without consideration. As I have told you, Katharine was my friend.

We left on a hot June day, the trees now thick with green. Katharine knew of a lake not far from the city where we could pay a small fee and spend the night. We pitched the tent there, near the car and a stucco structure with showers and bathroom stalls. The lake stretched out endlessly beneath the shadow of a mountain known as Mt. Rattlesnake. It was from the top of it, Katharine informed me, that we would toss her mother at sunrise.

That night we built a small fire and fried eggs.

Katharine sat on a tree stump and talked. She told me again of her mother, and her brother, who was missing in action in Korea. She told me about her father, whose belief in Jesus, she said, left no room for anything else, no place for a daughter and a son, not to mention a wife. "I can understand why she snapped," Katharine said. "I mean, think of how dull, no matter where. No one can live like that, in a fishbowl."

I sat and listened. The heat was god-awful. I had on the yellow nightgown. I had never worn it before; it seemed silly in the winter and when the weather turned warmer I entirely forgot. It was only while packing, reaching into an out-of-the-way drawer for my athletic socks, that I came upon it, crumpled into a silk ball, cocoon-like. I packed it who knows why; it was hot, as I have said, the night balmy in the way summer nights can be in places near Rochester, as if all the melted snow has been absorbed into the air, so heavy with it that your weight feels tripled. No matter. We fanned ourselves outside the strange tent and drank old fashioneds from a thermos that smelled of chicken soup. Katharine talked. She wore her bathing suit—the style popular at the time, polka-dotted, with a ruffled skirt—and her hair, that horse-brown color that is not at all ordinary, she had combed into a tight bun. I could see her through the just dark. I watched her hands, punctuating.

I do not entirely remember what happened next, how it came that the two of us, me in my yellow silk, Katharine in her bathing suit, wandered around the edge of the lake in the moon shadow of Mt. Rattlesnake. There was a tension about the evening, something awkward in the weather, as if a thunderstorm might erupt at any moment or lightning tear across the sky. Swallows behaved as bats, swooping about our heads, and frenzied balls of mosquitoes bred over the shallower parts of the lake water. At some point Katharine took my hand to stress something, and she did not let go.

Before I continue I should say that this was a time when women had clear boundaries, and even in discussion the boundaries were observed. Katharine had already broken down those boundaries between the two of us, and I believed her holding my hand as we walked the lakeshore trail was just a natural extension of all those afternoons together, lying jagged on her Persian rug. I don't know. I can tell you that the fireflies were thick and that the only sound we could hear across the lake was the sound of fish jumping. My silk nightgown felt light against my skin, damp from the humidity. It was not a weekend; there were no other campers. We were alone. Because of this, perhaps, we drew close, aware, as one becomes in certain moments, of the brevity of life.

After some time Katharine stopped and turned toward me. "Marion," she said, and put her hands on my shoulders. Her hair, as I have told you, was pulled back tight, and when she smiled her whole face seemed to lean into her mouth or radiate out from it in a way remarkable. Only her eyes were sad.

"You are my best friend," she said.

You are too young to understand what this once meant between women. No matter. I can tell you that there will be times when you have to choose between beginning again in a cold and lonely place or making do with whatever fragile shelter you have already built. I understood this, and knew that after that night I would never have another friend like Katharine, nor would I return to her house in the late afternoon or lean against her, back to back, to wish for spring. When she tried to kiss me I turned away. "I'm sorry" is what I said.

I slept that night outside and she slept in the tent. The flags hung limply. The next morning we woke before sunrise and climbed Mt. Rattlesnake. The top of the mountain was a collection of rocks, some moss-covered, some bare. From there we looked down at our tent, a miniature in the distance, and saw clearly the path we had walked the night before.

Katharine held the urn up high, intending to scatter her mother's ashes into the wind, but there was no wind and so the ashes simply fell into a heap on the rock on which we were standing. The two of us used branches to scrape them over the edge and then sat and watched the sun ascend. "I'm afraid she would have been displeased with me," Katharine said after some time. "I'm afraid she would have been horribly displeased. They all are, aren't they? Horribly displeased."

"I don't know," I said, and took her hand in mine. "No," I said.

Katharine died several years after we moved to Norfolk. I got the news over the telephone. We had lost touch, but that was not so unusual in those days when a woman stayed in a place only until her husband's next transfer. She had sent me Christmas cards, of course, and a longer note when she heard about your sister's birth. I still felt close to her in a way I've felt with no friend since, though after that excursion we saw each other rarely. Still, I waved whenever I drove down Country Club Road and passed her Tudor, forgetting that her windows were overgrown, imagining that she might be looking out, seeing me.

When Rick called, we were packing for Durham, getting things organized for the movers the next day. I had been feeling the nostalgia I have always felt on those eves of leaving. When I hung up the phone, I went back to what I had been doing, rolling china into sheaves of newspaper, marking cardboard boxes DEN, KITCHEN. I did not think of Katharine. Instead, I thought of the next neighborhood, the next house: how I would paint the living room walls, paper the bedrooms; how I would knock on the front doors of the houses on our new street, introducing myself, introducing you and your sister, accepting when the ones at home invited us in for tea and cookies. It felt somehow impossible to think of anything else, to think of the way she must have looked, so indiscreet, so inelegant, slumped against the steering wheel of that automobile going nowhere, idling in the garage over the long weekend Rick had chosen to take the boys camping. Instead, I pictured her in her coffin, pictured her in a yellow silk nightgown, because she always said things like silky nightgowns helped to chase away the blowsy feeling that came with every blue hour, when no man or beast, she said, should be left to swim alone.

PLAYDATE

Matilda's mother apologizes for calling so late, but she wonders whether Caroline might be free for a playdate? Like, tomorrow?

"Matilda's had a cancellation," she says.

Liz searches the kitchen drawer for Caroline's Week-at-a-Glance. It's ten already and she's had her wine; down the hall the baby nurse, Lorna, is asleep with the twins and Caroline; Ted's out of town. What the hell is Matilda's mother's name, anyway? Faith, Frankie, Fern—

"We could do an hour," Liz says. "We have piano at four-thirty."

She can picture her clearly: a single woman who hovers in the school hallways wearing the look that Liz has come to associate with certain mothers—a mixture of doe-eyed expectancy and absolute terror, as if at any minute they might be asked to recite the Pledge of Allegiance or the current policy on plagiarism; the school being one of those places where mothers are kept on their toes and organized into various committees for advance and retreat, their children's education understood as a mined battlefield that must be properly assaulted. Didn't she just see her last week at the enlightenment session? A talk given by a Dr. Roberta Friedman, Professor of

59

Something, entitled "Raising a Calm Child in the Age of Anxiety; or, How to Let Go and Lighten Up!" But now, for the life of her, Liz can't remember whether she and Matilda's mother exchanged two words, just the way Matilda's mother balanced on the edge of her folding chair taking notes, the intentional gray streak (intellectual?) of her cropped hair, the fury of her pen.

"Oh, God, that's great," Matilda's mother is saying. "I just need to keep Matilda from losing her gourd."

"I understand," Liz says.

"Do you?" says Matilda's mother. "You do?"

Her name is Fran, apparently. Fran Spalding. Liz has looked her up in the confidential, you-lose-it-you're-screwed Parent & Faculty directory. She and Matilda live across the park from the school, on West Eighty-sixth Street. Does anyone not live uptown? Liz wants to know, but she asks the question only of herself, so there's no answer, just the relative quiet of her studio—a big loft in what was once considered Chinatown. Liz spends most mornings here spinning clay into pots and teacups and dessert plates. At this hour there's little interruption, just the occasional rumble of a garbage truck and the low chatter of the radio and her own mind: Fran Spalding, daughter Matilda, West Eighty-sixth. They'll go today after school.

They'll cross the park in a taxi, mothers and daughters, and aim for the apartment building, three-forty-something, where Fran Spalding and Matilda live, and go up to the fifteenth floor, 15A, she knows—the address listed in the second section of the directory, the front pages clotted with emergency numbers and please-put-in-a-place-of-prominence evacuation routes.

It's a playdate, a date for play; Caroline duly apprised of the plan this morning as she and Liz waited for the school bus on Lafayette. Around them, Cooper Union students bunched up like blackflies, bluebottles in window corners, at every DON'T WALK.

"Who?" Caroline says.

"Matilda. She's in your class. You know. She wears striped shirts."

"Does she have a cat?" Caroline asks.

"I have no idea."

"Does she want to play My Little Ponies?"

Liz looks down at her daughter. "Who doesn't?" she says.

Caroline shoves her hands in her pockets and swings one leg. She leans against a filthy meter tattooed with stickers advertising things: 800 numbers for important advice; someone staying positive with HIV.

"I'll go," Caroline says, as if going were a question.

"Great!" Liz says. "Here comes the bus!"

The school bus is the big yellow kind, exactly the same as the one Liz once rode to elementary school, in that faraway place, that faraway land known as rural Ohio. Here, in lower Manhattan, the bus seems too large, wrong, a dinosaur lurching through the veering bicyclists and throngs of pedestrians, the construction cones and smoking manholes; a relic of a thing, a dirtied yellow shell, an empty chrysalis whose butterfly has flown the coop. Inside, a handful of children are spread front to back, their expressionless faces gazing out the smeared windows, their ears plugged. Her own school bus, her Ohio school bus, had burst with noise and the boys who wouldn't move over and then, later, would.

The bus stops; its doors open. Liz releases Caroline's hand and waits as she ascends the high steps and disappears down the aisle. In an instant, she reappears in the window seat closest to Liz, her backpack beside her like a twin. Liz waves and smiles; that she has refused to buy headphones and the machines into which they fit remains a constant source of outrage to her daughter, though on this morning Caroline seems happy enough, smiling back, crossing her eyes and sticking out her tongue as the doors close and the school bus lurches on.

"First, the golden rule: never compare your own childhood experiences with those of your children," Dr. Friedman had said, her glasses pushed to the tip of her nose. "This is a fruitless exercise, unhealthy and counterproductive. Best to remain alert; to look on the bright side; to, whenever possible, accentuate joy."

Liz pounds the clay on the wheel and straightens her miner's cap, a figment of her imagination but one that works relatively well in focusing her thoughts away from the business of children and onto the clay. The twins are presumably in the park with Lorna, sleeping in their double stroller or being pushed, side by side, in the swings meant for babies. Lorna is a pro. She will have bundled them up and thought to bring nourishment—formula or the breast milk that Liz pumps every evening; her breasts have nearly expired, she thinks, they've hit their expiration date. And Caroline is safely in school, repeating the colors of vegetables in Spanish or sitting at a small round table having what's known as Snack: individual packages of Cheez-Its (they've all complained!), or free-of-hydrogenated-oils-and-corn-syrup-though-possibly-manufactured-in-a-factory-traced-with-nuts animal crackers. The point is, Liz has five hours before she needs to take the subway uptown: five whole hours. It is nothing and everything. It could stretch out before her like an eternity if she has the will, or it could evaporate in a single moment.

Concentrate, she thinks.

In the bright light of the cap, Liz sees the spinning clay take form and her own hands, aged, fingernails bitten to the quick. She has written Fran Spalding's cell phone number across her knuckles, in case she forgets, or there's a problem, or the world blows its cork: a possibility, a probability, apparently, but for now she's going to concentrate. She's not going to think about that.

"Ladies and Gentlemen, this is an important message from the New York City Police Department," says the subway voice over the loudspeaker five hours later. Liz stands half in, half out of the subway car, a new habit; she always waits until the last passengers have pushed past before she fully commits to sitting down.

"Remain alert. Keep your belongings in your sight at all times. Protect yourself. If you see a suspicious package or activity on the platform or train, do not keep it to yourself. Tell a police officer or an MTA employee.

"Remain alert, and have a safe day," the voice adds as the doors shut.

The taxi barrels across Central Park, through its odd scattering of tunnels; blocks of stone rise on either side of the road as if the taxi were plummeting through earth. Above loom the barren trees, leafless and gray, or the blotched white of sycamores; once, aeons ago it seems now, orange flags were unfurled along this same route. Then, thousands of people, all of them vaguely smiling, had wandered the paths like pilgrims in a dream. No one appears to be smiling now. They hurry along, wrapped in their coats, the day leaden, darkening; an Ethan Frome day, Liz used to say in college, to be clever, though she wasn't particularly, unable to decipher the strange manners and customs of the East. She hasn't thought of that in years.

Fran pays the driver, while Liz, in back, unbuckles Caroline and Matilda, leaning over them to push open the door. "On the curb," she's saying. "Watch your step," she's saying. "Grab your gloves." Fran gestures for them to follow her into the building entrance, where two men in uniform hold open the large glass doors, bowing slightly as Fran passes.

"Partner!" one of them says, high-fiving Matilda. "Who's your buddy?"

"Michael," Fran says, arrested at the welcome threshold. "This is Matilda's friend Carolyn."

"Caroline," Liz says; she can't help it, raw nerve. Anything else she would let slide, she tells herself. Truly.

"Of course," Fran is saying. *"Caroline."*

"Buddy bear," Michael says to Matilda. "Look at you."

They look. How can they not? Everywhere there are mirrors, reflecting them, reflecting Michael and the other guy, reflecting the bounty and the grandeur of it all—potted green plants with white lights, garlands, a cone of poinsettia, and even, on a pedestal between the elevator banks, an elaborately carved stone urn containing—what? Liz wonders. Dead tenants?

"This is lovely," Liz says.

"It's home," Fran says. She rings for the elevator, the girls crowding next to her. In an instant there's the ping, and then the doors slide open. Another man in uniform smiles as they all step in; there is a small chair in the corner for sitting, though he clearly prefers to stand.

"Hey, Matty," he says. "How's the Go-Go?"

Go-Go, Fran explains, is the cat, their cat, who recently contracted a hot spot. A hot spot, she tells Liz, is an itch that can't be scratched.

"Wow," Liz says.

They rise in mechanical wonder and then stop, abruptly, on eleven, where the elevator doors slide open to no one.

"False alarm," the man in the uniform says, releasing the doors and driving them onward, upward. The girls stand stock still; they all stand stock still.

"Are you allergic?" Matilda says to Caroline.

"The cat," Fran says to Caroline.

"Are you allergic to cats?" Matilda says. She

wears pink plastic barrettes and a striped shirt underneath a pink jumper. "Caroline," Liz says. "Did you hear—"

"No," Caroline says. She hunches beneath her huge backpack, carried solely for fashion, or just in case. In it now, Liz happens to know, is a palm-size notepad on which Caroline draws the details of her day and a purple-lipsticked Bratz doll that she treasures, received on her last birthday from Ted's mother, who, Ted said, meant well.

"Lots of people are," Matilda says.

The elevator stops.

"North Pole," says the man in the uniform.

"Thank you," says Fran.

"Thank you," says Liz.

"Thank you," says Matilda.

"Thank you," says Caroline, walking behind Liz and tripping her, accidentally on purpose. "Caroline," Fran's voice soars in from ahead. "How do you feel about strudel?" But neither Caroline nor Matilda is listening, or hungry, for that matter; released from the grip of the elevator, the girls run down the poorly lit hallway playing some sort of imaginary game, knocking into doors and taking corners at high speed.

"Matilda Beth," Fran yells after them. "That's one." She pauses. "Don't let me get to two."

Matilda stops and grabs Caroline's hand, pulling her toward what must be A—an unassuming door with a child's drawing taped over its peephole. It is always the same, Liz thinks, in these pictures: the mismatched ears, the round eyes, the name scrawled across one corner. The girls are six years old and braided, the days of the week stitched on their underpants. They wear seamless socks and rubber-soled shoes, and both are missing two teeth, though not the same ones; each has been read *Charlotte's Web* and *The Boxcar Children*, the first a story of a pig on a farm and its friendship with a spider, the second a story of children, orphans, living happily alone in the woods, making do with rusted spoons pulled from the dump and the occasional cracked cup of milk.

"Caroline," Liz says. "Is this a gold-star day?" She has spied Caroline twisting her finger up her nose and refers to a deal between the two that sometimes results in better behavior but more often does not.

Once in the apartment, Matilda leads Caroline to her room, where they settle beneath a green canopy of gauze to play My Little Ponies. Liz returns to the living room with Fran, whose gray streak, she learns, is natural and who works at home during school hours, copyediting and proofreading documents for a legal firm. From time to time, the girls interrupt them, flying into the living room in leotards and ballerina skirts and, once, in nothing at all, at which point Fran calls Matilda aside and speaks to her in a voice that Liz has heard only from single mothers or from mothers with numerous children—women who simply do not have the time or the patience for the monkey business that everyone else puts up with, they have told her; once, even, she heard the voice from a mother who said she just placed herself in the hands of Jesus. So maybe it's the voice of Jesus, Liz thinks now, admiring it; her own, she knows, entirely lacks authority, as if she were questioning each verdict she pronounced.

"More tea?" Fran asks.

"Thank you," Liz says, following her back into the kitchen, where they wait with great anticipation for the water to boil, watching the kettle's curved spout, its shiny, smudged lid, as if they had never seen anything quite so fascinating in their lives.

"We are living in the Age of Anxiety," Dr. Friedman said, "and here we sit at the epicenter, the Ground Zero, if you will." She looked up and over those glasses at all of them, the throng of mothers, the few stay-at-home dads or those fathers whose schedules allowed them to be flexible—men in T-shirts, shorts, and sturdy boots, their hairy legs oddly comforting, as if, at a moment's notice, they could sweep the whole group onto their shoulders and hoist them out the window. Many of the women in the circle appeared to Liz to be close to tears, though some were more difficult to read, writing with expensive pens, their briefcases balanced against their slim ankles, their hair blown smooth. Dr. Friedman surveyed the room, clearly attempting to make eye contact with the closest suspect, though unfortunately that suspect was Janey Filch, wall-eyed and so shy she looked ready to faint.

"Everywhere we go are reminders of where we are. I don't think they need to be chronicled here. The school has briefed you on contingencies, and your emergency-contact cards have been filed in triplicate. Each child has an individual first aid kit and a protective mask.

"Still and still, you might say, the question remains: what can you do right now, on this day, at this hour, in this moment?"

Here Dr. Friedman looked up again and smiled, the smile so studied as to be disarming, as if Liz weren't really looking at a woman smiling but at a portrait of a woman smiling.

"Take a deep breath," she said, exhaling loudly. "Smell the roses," she said, inhaling loudly. "Relax."

The women slouched a bit in their folding chairs, attempting to follow Dr. Friedman's advice. Liz imagined that if Dr. Friedman were next to suggest that they all stand and do a few jumping jacks, most would leap to the job.

"Now," Dr. Friedman said, wiggling her shoulders. "I'm going to give you all some homework. This is an exercise that I've found works very well with my patients. It's simple, really. How many of you keep a journal?"

A few hands shot up, Marsha Neuberger waving as if desperate to be picked.

"That's fine, that's fine," Dr. Friedman said. "I only wanted to get an idea. Anyway, what I'm going to suggest is that you all try keeping what I call an anxiety journal; just like if any of you have ever tried to diet and kept a food journal—"

Anxiety journal like food journal, Liz would have written in her notes, if she had remembered paper and pen. Bemused laughter, she would have added.

"—where you wrote down your caloric intake. Your anxiety journal will be the place where you write down everything that makes you feel nervous, or anxious, throughout the day: it can be anything you like. Don't worry about how it sounds. No one is going to read it but you." This Dr. Friedman said emphatically, Liz would have noted, whipping off her glasses and looking up, avoiding Janey Filch but generally trying to reassure each and every one of them.

"Promise," she added.

Liz looks from her steaming tea to Fran. Fran is describing her terrific luck in finding the apart-

71

ment, falling into it, desperate, after fleeing San Francisco with Matilda and a few pieces of luggage. Now, as a single mother, she keeps a tight rein on things, she says. "Have you noticed?"

Liz is unsure whether she should have noticed or not, so she blows on her tea and shakes her head.

"There was a burglary," Fran says. "In San Francisco. After that we felt like we had to get out. I mean, I did. I left Matilda's father. Richard. And moved back East."

"Oh."

"Strudel?" Fran says, sliding a plate across the counter.

"Oh, gosh, no thanks."

"I've sliced some apples for the girls."

"Great," Liz says, knowing that Caroline won't touch them—the edges, minutes after being sliced, too brown.

"And you?" Fran says.

"I'm sorry?"

"What about you?" Fran says.

"Oh," Liz says. "We moved from Boston. We were in art school, Ted and I, and then we moved here—Ted works in television, children's television—and then we had Caroline and now the twins, but I'm getting back to it. Art. I'm a potter, actually. I work with clay."

"In vitro?" asks Fran.

"I'm sorry?"

"The twins," Fran says. "In vitro?"

Liz nods.

"Your eggs?"

Liz blows on her tea. "Nope. We had to shell out twenty thousand dollars; we did it through the alumni association."

"Smart eggs," Fran says.

"I didn't really care. Ted felt strongly about that, you know. He didn't want to adopt."

"Men rarely do."

They sit in the living room, on opposite sides of the sectional.

"I think our girls really get along," Fran says.

"Yes," Liz says.

"After the burglary, you know, Matilda had trouble making friends. I mean, she played by herself most of the time. Made up stories. I'd take her to a birthday party or something, and there all the other children would be running around and screaming and playing tag or smacking the piñata, that kind of thing, and Matilda would be sitting by herself involved in some fairy-tale game. It was, well, embarrassing, frankly."

Liz can't help thinking that taupe is entirely the wrong color for this room, high as they are above the city. Excellent light, the listing would say. Light and air; airy light; sun-drenched, sun-gorged, sun-soaked, rush to your sun-kissed oasis! There are windows everywhere, and those radiators that line the walls. Fran should clear them off and paint the place—something dramatic, terra-cotta, she'd suggest, or saffron yellow.

"This was in San Francisco, where everything is, well, healthy, do you know what I mean? There's always someone talking about loving-kindness. I couldn't stand it after a while. I just left. I mean, we did; after the burglary. We just got on a plane and flew away. Anyway, that's it. I'm here for good. I mean, I grew up here, in the city, but it's different now, of course. It's a lot different."

There is a bit of a pause; comfortable enough, Liz thinks. The truth is, she's enjoying herself. It's a playdate, she finds herself thinking; I'm on a date for play.

"Would you like a drink?" Fran says.

"A drink?"

"I'd have one if you would. Carpe diem, or whatever. Anyway, screw tea, we're grown-ups, right?"

"Okay," Liz says. "Sure. Great. Yes."

"Excellent!" Fran says.

From behind Matilda's door comes a shriek of giggles.

"Besides, they're having fun!" Fran says.

"So are we!" Liz says.

Fran disappears to the kitchen and Liz stands to stretch a bit, to look out the windows. The apartment faces west, she believes, though she gets turned around at these heights. She still isn't used to apartment views or high floors, and the ease with which you can see other lives: how even now, across from here, a boy sits reading at a dining room table while an old woman—a nurse? a grandmother? a nanny?—moves around him, straightening up, stepping in and then out of Liz's sight. A diorama, they are; what you might see at the American Museum of Natural History: early twenty-first century, NYC, USA. They're dead, actually—stuffed mammals, the old woman on some sort of a moving track.

And what of Fran in the kitchen? Liz in the living room? Urban/suburban women circa 2007 participating in/on playdate, an urban/suburban ritual intended to alleviate boredom/loneliness among children/women while encouraging/controlling social engagement—

"What?" Liz yells.

"Chilled?" Fran yells.

"Wonderful," Liz yells. She turns away from the windows; there are other things to do. She pokes around the taupe room. On a wide bookshelf are the usual histories and paperbacks and framed photographs: an infant Matilda; an earnest-looking boy in mortarboard and gown, Richard?; a teenage Fran leaning against a giant redwood, her hair not yet streaked with gray but solely black, her posture sophisticated, worldly—

she's in college, possibly, or a Manhattan high school. I live on a narrow island, her posture says. I live at the center of the world.

On the secretary are bills and Post-it notepads and loose receipts and whatnot. Liz has a strong feeling, a hot spot, an itch to be scratched, and, sure enough, there it is among them: Fran's anxiety journal. It's as she expected, a steno notebook generally used for reportage. Liz resists for only a moment.

"Voilà!" Fran says. Liz turns to see her carrying a tray, the TV-dinner kind; it makes Liz anxious.

"What have you got?" Fran says. She's pouring and doesn't notice.

"Oh, nothing," says Liz. "Your anxiety journal."

Fran stops. "You were reading it?"

"Oh, God, no. Of course not. I just saw it here and picked it up. I mean, I was thinking, Good for you, and remembering that I've been meaning to buy one, or get one. I'd write, 'TV-dinner tray.'"

"What?"

" 'TV-dinner tray.' Like the one you're holding. It makes me nervous and I can't tell you why."

Fran looks down. "It belonged to Richard. He liked to eat in front of the news."

"Exactly."

"Maybe it's the news you associate it with."

"Maybe."

"See? She had a point," Fran says. "Cheers!"

They toast and sip the wine, which is delicious chilled, Liz says—she never thinks to do that. "You should," Fran says. She takes the anxiety journal and tucks it beneath one of the sectional cushions. "To playdates!" she says, toasting again.

It's near the dinner hour and the girls are getting hungry; they haven't heard a peep from their mothers. Pinkie Pie and Sun Sparkles have been to the castle about a zillion times; they've flown in the blue balloon, late for the costume ball, and then arrived, the My Little Pony theme song playing as Pinkie Pie and Sun Sparkles twirl on the special pink plastic revolving disk within the castle walls. Caroline lies on her back, pedaling her legs in the air, her finger working her nose. Matilda is reprimanding her imaginary sister, Beadie.

"Get down from there," Matilda says. Beadie perches dangerously close to the window ledge, threatening to jump, and even though she has wings on her back and little ones at her ankles, Matilda pleads with her to stop.

"Goodbye, my friend," Beadie says. "Goodbye!"

Beadie takes a tremendous leap and falls, tumbling, toward the street. Matilda screams an imaginary scream, though Beadie, she knows, won't splat; she'll fly with her little wings right back to Matilda's room. Still, Matilda feels scared.

"Help! Help!" Matilda yells. "Thief! Help! Thief!"

The door swings open.

"Do not even start with that," Fran says. "It makes me insane." Behind Fran, Liz looks in. "Caroline," she says. "Gold-star day, remember?"

Caroline pulls her finger out of her nose.

"Are you girls happy?" Fran says.

"We're hungry," they say.

"We're staying for dinner, how's that!" Liz says.

The girls hop up and down holding hands; they wear only their underwear.

Chicken nuggets are served. Somewhere in Matilda's room, Fran is saying as she prepares the tray, live a round table and two chairs, Little Bear size, ordered from one of those catalogues which arrive daily in the mail; this one featured three child models, she's saying, two girls and one boy, sipping tea at the table, sunlight streaming through windows that looked out on what appeared to be Russian countryside. The girls were dressed beautifully; the boy served in a monogrammed apron. Or maybe it came from the other one, Fran says, knocking on the door, the one where the child models introduced themselves and listed their goals. "I'm Zelda,"

Fran says in a wavery falsetto. "I'm going to be a rock star." Fran opens the door; inside, the girls huddle within the gauzy tent, apparently hiding.

"I can't remember which," Fran continues, "but the point is, it's really cute, and it cost a fortune, and it must be here somewhere. I mean, you can't just lose a table and chairs."

Fran wades through stuffed animals and clothes and artwork and books, to a stack of pillows and blankets in the center of Matilda's room, excavating until she finds the ensemble buried beneath. They were making a fort.

"Jesus," she says, flushed. "Can you believe all this crap?"

"Yes," Liz says.

Fran sets down the tray and calls the girls over. "Okay, ladies," she says. "Which princess?"

"Jasmine," Matilda says.

"Oh, for God's sake," Fran says, rotating the plates.

"Ketchup?" Liz says; she holds the bottle at the ready. The girls nod, and she lurches toward them, ready to squirt.

"I can't say that anything really happened with Richard," Fran says. "It was just, you know, the feeling." She lies on the floor in the now dim light of the apartment, balancing her wineglass on her chest, her feet propped on the sectional. "The elephant-in-the-room feeling."

79

"The wha?" Liz says. She can't remember the last time she drank so much wine in the afternoon; usually, she waits until Caroline's asleep, the twins with Lorna in the nursery, Ted back at the office (the demanding life of a children's television executive!) before pouring her first glass. Then she might have another, and another, enough to erase the day, or the parts of it she doesn't want to remember: Caroline standing with her backpack on Lafayette, the neon-scrawled windows of the gay bar next to the bus stop, the public-service poster of an unattended bag, like an old-fashioned doctor's bag, shoved beneath some unsuspecting person's seat.

"The elephant-in-the-room feeling," Fran says. "You know, the thing that's just, God, there. It's big and heavy and real, somehow, though unnamed. It's just there, is all, this blob of feeling; the feeling from the Black Lagoon."

Fran rolls over on one elbow. "Did you ever ruin your life for a feeling?" she says.

"I don't know," Liz says. "I hope not." She has closed her eyes to watch the tiny red pricks of light behind her eyelids. It's a trick she likes to do, a habit; she likes to count them, pretend they're sparks. She's combustible, perhaps—she's burning up.

"I miss Richard," Fran is saying. "I miss him every day. There's nobody to tell anything to anymore. Nobody."

Liz opens her eyes and the sparks die out; she is back where she was, things reassembling around her—bookshelf, secretary, radiator, carpet, floor lamps.

"I mean, there never was anybody to talk to, really," Fran is saying. "But there sort of was. I thought there was. For a while I used to. Do you know what I mean?"

"Yes," Liz says, closing one eye and then the other; it changes her perspective. "I think so," she says. She is a highly trained artist, she could tell you. She has training up the wazoo. She got a fellowship, even, and there were many, many applicants. She majored in art history, in case you're interested.

"Do the others look like you?" Fran asks.

"What?" Liz says.

"The twins. Do they look like you? Or, you know, like the smarter, younger egg woman?"

Liz laughs. She doesn't mean to, but she laughs and tips over the wineglass that she forgot she'd balanced beside her. There's just a little left, just a drizzle to darken an already wet spot; she's a well-trained klutz is what she is, a social miscreant fluent in art history, trained in art history. "Sorry, sorry," she says. "I did it again."

"Forget it," Fran says.

Liz blots the wet spot with her shirtsleeve. "Not at all is the thing," she says. "The twins don't look like either of us. They're blond and blue-eyed, for one. I mean, adorable. Absolutely adorably wonderful, but people think they're adopted."

"That's so funny," Fran says.

"I forgot to laugh," Liz says.

"But you're lucky," Fran says.

"God, I know," Liz says. "I am in the ninety-ninth percentile of luck."

"You tested out," Fran says.

"I am among the gifted and talented."

From Matilda's room there's the sound of a thud.

"You guys happy?" Fran yells.

"We're okay!" Matilda yells back.

"Caroline?" Liz yells.

"Yes?"

"Are you still there?"

"I'm here," Caroline says.

"I thought she might have disappeared," Liz says. "Sometimes I think she'll just disappear."

"They're fine," Fran says. "More?"

"Just a skosh," Liz says.

"A skosh?" Fran says.

"Japanese for 'a little,' " Liz says. "Sukoshi."

"Oh," Fran says. "Do you speak it?"

"My dad was in the service. Stationed there. I used to think it was Yiddish. He'd say 'Just a skosh' whenever you offered him wine. I miss him, too," Liz says. "Like Richard."

"Your dad?"

"Yes."

"Here." Fran pours; they've finished one bottle and opened another. What they are celebrating they have no idea.

"Lemme at it," Liz says. She crawls along the sectional on all fours. She hasn't been able to locate the floor lamp switch, but it doesn't matter; she's a cat who can see in the dark. "It was here, I saw it. You took it away from me."

"Oh, God!" Fran shrieks. "The whole thing is so stupid. Please."

"Lemme, lemme, lemme," Liz says.

"You're going to hate me," Fran says.

"Are you kidding?" Liz says. "You're my new best friend."

"You have to promise," Fran says.

"I promise, I promise," Liz says.

"Not to laugh. Really. No. I mean it. Don't laugh. You're going to laugh. I know it. I can just—"

"Bluebird's honor," Liz says. "Bluebird, Brownie, Girl Scout, Kappa Kappa Gamma. God, can you believe me?"

"Wow," Fran says. "Are you serious?"

"I'm always serious," Liz says. "I'm never not serious. I'm a never-not-serious Ohioan, Ohioette gal, aren't I? I remain alert."

"Do you think if we lived there or, like, Montana or something, things would be, I don't know, different?" Fran says.

"Ta-da!" Liz says.

"Shit," Fran says.

"I found it!" Liz says.

"Shit," Fran says.

"You said I could."

"Go ahead, just please. You promised."

"I'll be dead serious," Liz says. She swings her bare feet around. "I am dead serious," she says. "I am a deadly serious, dead-serious, never-not-serious person. I repeat, I remain alert."

What is she saying? She has no idea, really, though it feels good to speak, the words tumbling out of her mouth and knocking around in the darkening room, high above the city where she has spent the afternoon with a new friend, a sophisticated friend, a woman who grew up here, a woman with a streak of natural gray, a divorced single mother with a legal, razor-sharp mind who can look down on the lights and know where she is, know all the cross streets and the avenues, know the best places to buy things, the best things to buy, a woman who used to bicycle to Greenwich Village, who met Bob Dylan, even, in one of those places where people met Bob Dylan, back when the Village was the Village, and Bob Dylan lived there, or, at least, sang there, but then that would have been Fran's mother, maybe, or an older brother who didn't mind Fran tagging along, who took her even, rode with her balanced on his handlebars. And now look!

This! The promise of the journal in her hands! Fran made notes! She caught all the things that Liz missed—the meeting room overheated and crowded, the acoustics so bad it was impossible to concentrate. And afterward—this is now Liz talking, Liz continuing to talk, Liz babbling—Dr. Friedman had been so mobbed, so impossible to get to, that she had actually waited in the school lobby and followed her out, down Madison and then some, then over, to Lexington, the subway entrance there, Dr. Friedman walking with such robotic—

"What?" Fran says. "What?"

"Robotic," Liz says.

"Oh," Fran says. "Right, robotic. Go on."

—purpose, that she quite literally couldn't catch up. She just couldn't catch up, she says again, before Dr. Friedman flew down the stairs to the subway.

"A flying robot," Fran says.

Liz turns to the journal. "It must be done," she says. "The consensus has been reached."

"Okay," says Fran, who has moved to sit cross-legged on the floor in front of her.

"It won't hurt," Liz says.

"Please."

"Well, just a little."

"Thank you."

"I'll make it quick," Liz says.

"All right," Fran says.

"These are difficult times, terrible times. Someone's got to police the world."

Liz opens the journal to read, but the truth is, it's difficult to see what's written in the near dark, and her eyes have started to go. She brings the page to her face, and squints:

1. Crowds
2. School
3. Shadows
4. Playdates
5. Lunchrooms
6. Anniversaries

"What?" Fran's saying. "What? Oh, God. What did I write?" She moves closer to Liz, scoots in, so that Liz imagines Fran might next crawl into her lap as Caroline does, settle there between her legs to practice reading in the way she's been instructed at school: Read It Once to See; Read It Twice to Comprehend; Read It Again to Fully Absorb Its Meaning.

Go-Go appears from nowhere. He scratches and scratches, biting at the hot spot on his leg, gnawing. "Stop!" Fran says, clapping her hands. "Stop!"

Liz closes the journal and stands up a bit unsteadily. "Jesus, it's dark," she says. "I can't believe it got so late." She hands the journal to Fran. "I promised Lorna I'd be back earlier."

"Right," Fran says, taking the journal. "God, I'm sorry."

"Oh, no. This was fun. I mean, this was really fun, and the girls—"

"They seem to hit it off," Fran says.

"Caroline!" Liz yells in the direction of Matilda's room, the shut door. "Shit. We had piano. I totally forgot."

"Oh, my God. I'm really sorry," Fran says. "I started—"

"Don't apologize. Caroline hates piano. Anyway, it wasn't your—are these my shoes?"

"Here," Fran says. "They're here, with Caroline's backpack."

"Caroline!" Liz yells.

"It's impossible to get them—"

"Caroline, now!"

The door opens slowly and the girls, or what looks like shadows of the girls, drift out, fall out, into the hallway.

"Are Thursdays better?" Fran is saying.

"I'm sorry?"

"Thursdays. We could do Thurs—"

Liz feels a kind of draining away, as if the ebb of the twilight has returned to the night all that is loose, unmoored. She has always fought the feeling of this time of day, when her father would remain in the garden and her mother did what mothers did then in the house. Liz would ride her bike up and down the driveway, waiting for her father to call her, to tell her to come quick, to come see the misshapen gourd, or the earthworm, or the potato bug before it got too dark, and she would, before it went black as pitch. She would hurry, she would pedal like the wind to get to what her father held: this thing unknown, random, discovered in the dirt and now there for her in her father's hand. A miracle. It's what placed her squarely in the world, what kept her from being sucked out.

"Yes," Liz says. "Sure, whatever." She ties up Caroline's sneakers, yanks the laces tight. "I'm sorry about Richard," she says, straightening.

"Oh, it's fine," says Fran. "Really. Matilda and I are a team, aren't we, Matty?"

"Rah-rah," Liz says.

"Thursdays," Fran says. She has found Caroline's jacket beneath the coatrack and now holds it out for her. "We're going to do Thursdays!" she says to Matilda.

"Let me check at home," Liz says. "I never know which end is up."

"Oh," Fran says.

"Thank Matilda," Liz says to Caroline.

"Thank you," Caroline says.

"Thank Fran," Liz says.

"Thank you," Caroline says.

Liz clutches Caroline's hand on the subway platform. There is work being done somewhere, and the trains are running intermittently, though a taxi or a bus is out of the question—the traffic insane. The twins have had their baths and are sleeping, Liz has heard from Lorna. Everything is fine, she has been told.

"Ladies and Gentlemen," booms the intercom. "This is an important message from the New York City Police Department. Remain alert. Keep your belongings in your sight at all times. Protect yourself. If you see a suspicious—"

"Did you have a good time?" Liz says, talking over the recorded voice, squatting so that she can be at eye level with the girl.

"Uh-huh," Caroline says.

"Is Matilda nice?" Liz says.

"Uh-huh," Caroline says.

"Does she like to play My Little Ponies?" Liz says.

Caroline pulls on the loose straps of her backpack, a filched Pinkie Pie, its tail braided, its eyes pocked by a pen point, now zipped into one of the many compartments.

"I don't know," Caroline says. She turns away from her mother and stares out over the empty tracks. "No," she adds quietly, though who could hear anything for the screech of the approaching train. In the rush Liz teeters, grabbing Caroline into a hug, her hands gripping Caroline's thin shoulders for balance. "But it was a gold-star day, baby," she says as the crowd swells over them. "Wasn't it?"

ESPERANZA

The point is she had almost lost Baby in Chile. They had jabbed a needle in her rear—progesterone or estrogen, testosterone, something—and the needle, true story, broke off. Broke! How they ever got the thing out she'll never know because she fainted dead away. And Chile wasn't then what it is now, no; dogs, mostly, scrawny, ugly packs of them on every corner. Children, too, little more than five, six, selling roped iguana and necklaces of dried corn dyed berry reds and blues, and one boy, she'll never forget, with half a pack of cards splayed on the ground as if he were playing solitaire, but he was not: they were for *sale*. He had worked out an elaborate system of value; spades cost the most though she would have thought hearts.

Wouldn't that have been poetic? Hearts?

She had offered him a quarter for a four of diamonds. It seemed a card of no worth and she didn't want to deplete his inventory; plus a quarter then and so forth. The value. He spit on the coin and polished it against his ragged shirt. He was a beautiful child. He had those enormous Latin eyes. She had wanted to fold him up and carry him home in her pocket—women did back then. They simply took a child home. A friend's brother was just a boy from down the street, a boy who had walked in—a prostitute sister, a drunk dad, something—and one morning the boy had just walked into her friend's apartment, this is New York City, Hell's Kitchen, the Irish, you know, anyway, the boy had walked in or banged on the door or something and her friend's mother had offered him eggs and made a place at the table. You *shared,* was the point. You didn't need written permission. Not like now. No. *Compassion* was the point.

But your father said no. Don't steal the urchins, your father said. The vagabond of Mesoamerica. He said things he found clever and she did too though not in hindsight. Hindsight twenty-twenty and Dick still Dick even though and is this true? Did she hear correctly that he now prefers *Richard?* Changing at his age! Fathering twins! Outrageous when Baby clocked in at thirty-two.

"Thirty-three," Baby corrects.

Thirty-three? Already? Thirty-three? That's impossible. This is that many years ago? God knows the needle might still be in her rump, shrapnel from a war wound. Hah! She never saw them take it out but then again, how would she? She'd fainted dead away; felt the gurney roll as she hit the sheet and this is what she last remembers, the hormones surging through her body, buffering the pull that had come on too early for Baby to be born, the countergravity, perhaps, below the equator. Who knows? She had already lost four, remember? This might have been a big family instead of just the three of them.

"A perfect triumvirate of love," Baby says.

What?

"Iris Murdoch. The writer. She was an only child. She called her family a 'perfect triumvirate of love.' I read it."

Well, it wasn't for lack of trying! She had always imagined a room full of children, a fire in the grate with some kind of weather, and woods to roam.

"I know."

The first happened so early she hadn't even noticed. In those days you didn't keep such close track. The others were later, harder, after your father and I had already imagined them into children: a girl or a boy, brown eyes or blue, fair complexion most likely, given Dick's coloring, mine, and athletes, of course. Intelligence mattered less then—things had a way of working out. Health, always health first: ten fingers ten toes, that sort of thing. This before they had the pictures. You couldn't look in, couldn't know anything for sure. You had to have faith and you did, my God! The truth is, in those days you might very well have given birth to a swan or a rodent. And listen to this: now they can even grade the embryos. They give you the odds based on one cell—there are eight and they take one and test it and then give you the odds about the embryo's survival, its future, its earning power.

"I know."

It's not supposed to hurt anything, but how do they know? Might be the central trauma of the child's life: its lost cell.

"Seven is a lucky number."

The point is we got on the first plane home and my rump was so sore I had to sit on one of those inflatable cushions and traveling wasn't then what it is now, no, and oh, you're tired, never mind.

She had told the story so many times. She could see she is boring her, anyway.

"No."

Same old, same old.

"It's like water, or waves: I find it soothing."

What would she rather talk about?

"Nothing."

All right, then: nothing. Quiet as a mouse.

Baby closes her eyes and shifts down in her chair. She wears the pale blue gown she's been given on admittance, though *gown* is a charitable word. The cloth might as well be paper for its stiffness, the way it rustles. She wears the issued slippers. Next visit she might be able to receive certain things from home, her studio, a fifth-floor walk-up on Downing Street, where she's lived for the past twelve years above the guy who practices the viola at 4:00 p.m. and the woman who cries. The woman who cries only cries on the weekends, early Sunday mornings. It is not clear she's in trouble, but it is not clear she's not. Baby has not known what to do with this and so has done nothing. This is one of the things she's been talking about in session; she's also been talking about the man who fell in front of the bus on Avenue A, and the pigeons she feeds when she sits on the bench outside the Little Red School House. She has not been talking about the burn marks on her arms or how, weeks before she arrived, she lit matches and scorched the ends of her hair, her tongue.

This is the room where they let them smoke, a room not unlike the clinic in Chile, apparently, windowless, barrack-like. Her mother has brought flowers she's picked from the side of the highway, Queen Anne's lace and some other wild something that grows in June, a geranium or maybe even a lupine, stalky and purple. She brought them in a mason jar she filled with water from the drinking fountain; but there's nowhere to put them so she holds them in her lap, steadying the mason jar with both hands.

The cigarette burns down in the ashtray. Baby hasn't smoked in years but she loves the look of the column of papery ash and she loves the smoking room for its emptiness, its quiet, its walls a color that might have once been bright, who knows? Anyway, she might smoke. She might reach out and pick up the cigarette and take a long drag to see the look on her mother's face, but she won't, just as she won't interrupt her mother; won't eat between meals; won't stop scratching the itch; won't stop plucking the eyelashes from her eyelids; she won't.

Her father had barely said a word. He sat in this same room as a cigarette burned down in this same ashtray but he did not tell stories of when she was a child, or how lucky she was to be born, or of the afternoon she was forgotten at the beach, how her mother had thought Baby had been strapped in the back seat and her father had thought Baby had been strapped in the back seat and the two of them had driven not so far away but still, but still, turning in to the hotel and parking in the parking lot and the back seat empty, the back seat empty! Baby now holding the hand of a stranger, a woman with four kids of her own who had noticed the toddler plunked on the curb, teary, picking at a scab, and bought her an ice cream and sat to wait exactly where she was lost for her to be found because she would always be found, the stranger had said, her parents would always be on their way, she promised; instead, her father had said nothing and then cleared his throat or put down his newspaper and talked about his toddler twins, Brie and Brian, her half sister and half brother, and the way in which they already finished each other's sentences and seemed to speak in a language all of their own creation. He sat very straight and tall in his bucket seat, its plastic veined in black. Someone had left a Styrofoam cup of tobacco juice on the floor and leaving he had accidentally knocked it over. The stain still there if you looked for it. Baby opened her eyes to look for it and there it was, just beneath her mother's espadrille. Funny. It took the shape of South America.

Baby's name isn't truly Baby. It is Esperanza; ridiculous, given her Nordic ancestors and coloring, but Esperanza nonetheless. It just seemed the right thing to do considering the quick thinking of the Chilean doctors, the needle dose of hormone that prevented her from slipping out too soon and almost never being born after all the years her parents had waited for her. She was Espy at school, suitably short and vague in heritage—a name that made you think of white shirts and perpetual tans, summer sailing trips of the kind the family took in the years when they were flush, skirting the coasts of ravaged countries whose names ran together as the names of the muses or the many children of Zeus—mellifluous and full. Islands sprung whole from a woolly head, their namesakes the results of rapes or brutal kidnappings, the landscapes far too exotic and dangerous to enter but they would anchor off their rocky coasts and swim in the crystalline waters. They would fish for briny lobster or a local edible: a perfect triumvirate of love.

Baby shifts in her chair. The cigarette has burned to ash, the smoke dissipating then disappeared to nothing but its sharp smell. Her mother looks toward where a window might be if a window had ever been planned. Perhaps she is imagining what it might look out to: the industrial park off the industrial drive, the pretty apple trees planted in a semicircle around the hospital sign, the various persons wandering the grounds with their daughters—the facility for women, alone—some unsteady, some striding, manic.

Her mother is trying to be quiet as a mouse, Baby can see; but this is not her mother's nature. Her mother sees her noticing and smiles, her hands in a jumble of wild flowers, her scarf bright. She has put on fresh lipstick just that morning, or perhaps in the car, in the rearview mirror, before getting out and locking the door, before walking in with the quick steps Baby always heard before any others, the quick steps of mother, the click clack of mother, the voice of mother.

It will be over in an instant, she says now: a chatty mouse. They put the things on and then they take them off.

Her mother smiles and steadies the mason jar in her lap.

There's really nothing to be afraid of, she says.

Afterward, she strokes Baby's hair, smooths it away from her face, which is puffy and mottled white, not an easy face to love—the drugs they've given Baby make her furry and dark, a mustache across her top lip, random hairs on her cheeks so she must shave with a razor every morning like a man. In family group, Baby says she wishes she had never been born, but here she is, here she is! Sleeping soundly at last. She will sleep for many hours, the doctor has said, and when she wakes up she will feel better. That is what's been promised: Baby will feel better.

She fingers a small curl, staring at her child as she did when she was first born, as if she might swallow her whole. Then she could not sleep for watching Baby breathe: this miracle she had been given: this found girl.

TO DO

Her mother had been a beauty, a green-eyed blonde who wore a long braid down her back in high school and then college (Vassar '53), New York, and her job in the typing pool at Westinghouse (Katie Gibbs '54), before she was asked (actually, *told*) to change to the more stylish updos of the time. She refused, her boss accusing her of hysteria though the origin of the word *(do you know this?)* is the once-belief that the uterus could reach up its bloody hands and grip the throat.

Constance addresses the mostly silent women, colleagues from her department, gathered in the Antler Bar on Elm, near the Loop, for the new Storytelling Wednesdays, the audience's silence not silence but agitated, bored distraction as Constance closes with a recitation of her mother's to-do list, one of many she found among her mother's things last spring upon her mother's passing, she's explained. Cirrhosis of the liver but that's another story.

This list was picked at random from one of the drawers in the condo kitchen, her mother in one of those retirement communities haunted by women and men at the end stage, although who ever saw the men? The men were parked in different hallways—narrow, wallpapered corridors lined with geraniums, Constance says, miles and miles of geraniums, she says, the wallpapered walls hung with Wyeth and Rockwell and Turner prints, the corridors labyrinthine, windowless. I was always lost, she tells the silent women. The staff gave me three weeks to clear everything out. Presto pronto, Goodwill hello. No condolences. And these *lists*. Everywhere: on the backs of envelopes and cardboard coasters, pharmaceutical notepads, Post-its in different colors, and scraps of watercolor paper, she likes to paint, *liked* to paint, and anyway, everything. So much to do. Lists and lists.

The crowd's silence is the same weight she senses in class sometimes when she wanders to a different topic, or at a dinner table when she's had too much wine.

"I call it," she says, clearing her throat, "To Do. I hope everyone will get the picture," she adds as someone scrapes her chair back and angles toward the bathroom. The others watch her progress, riveted.

A few performers later, Beth, Constance's colleague, stands bare-chested, center stage, spoons balanced on her nipples, her medium essentially visual, she had said. We would do it at football parties, she said. It was a thing. And now here a visual reimagining of my lost youth, she said, unbuttoning, killing the same crowd, the women wildly applauding as Beth looks up, her face flushed even from this distance or perhaps it's the lights: they flood the makeshift stage, flood Beth, the glare of them casting Beth as something other, something more. Is she wearing face paint? Has she grown a third eye? One silver spoon drops to the floor and the crowd, collectively, gasps.

Her mother's To Do went something like this: bleach; *yarn;* Q-tips?; blueberries?; call Constance; organize girls; ask William. Constance had read each item slowly, deliberately, clarifying a few details—William her mother's ex-husband, Constance's father, long deceased; girls she and her younger sister, Sally, she supposed, all the while thinking, even while reading, What was I thinking? What was I thinking?

Her performance had lasted no more than a few minutes but the weight had solidified into a rock you might split open with a hammer and chisel.

It all had to do with *saying* something, Constance had told herself; continuity and mothers; lists and identity. In short: are we the sum of what we've crossed off? Or, are we only what we still have left to do? Her mother's death wasn't the point. People died every week at that place, every day of the year. Mothers. Fathers. In her mother's retirement community they printed—*embossed*—the names of the newly dead on ivory card stock each morning and propped the card as if a menu on a tiny easel outside the dining room. Dinner specials, her mother had called them. *Death du jour.*

When Constance visited, which she did less often than she would like to admit, she steered her mother clear of the easel and wheeled her straight to the employee who manned the dining room door. "We have a standing reservation," her mother would say, a joke, or, coquettishly, "Table for two."

Now Constance gestures to the waitress for another drink; she wants it quickly before the loudly applauded Beth returns, although Beth appears to be going nowhere, the audience whistling as if to summon dogs. Earlier Beth had ordered a green tea and a warm quinoa with kale. Protein and grains, she explained, and no to wine, thanks—one glass will make her fuzzy-headed in the morning and Beth wants none of *that,* she's having none of that, apparently. She had smiled. Sorry, she said. I'm a boring date.

Where is camaraderie? Constance wants to know. What happened to camaraderie? To nights out? To bonding? To drunkenness? All these young women so lean and muscular and accomplished at thirty, ivy leagued, Brazilian waxed, thonged, tattooed. She pictures even her little sister, Sally, thonged, tattooed, bending down to wipe the chin of one of her numerous children. Tattooed! Sally! Jesus!

Antlers is a university bar, odd downtown, off the Loop with its streets of neon pizza establishments and old Polish restaurants, marble-floored, near-embalmed waiters, odd so close to the lake, where on certain nights, such as this one, the wind tunnels down Sheridan, up Oak, pummeling the glass-wrapped new condos and bending near to snap the pear trees planted in boxes on Oak, and Willow, and Maple. Here Antlers's many-mullioned windows seem oblivious to weather, the glass plastered with peeling team mascots and political stickers, the walls dense with important persons in black and white, most already forgotten, their capped smiles wide and white, their hairstyles the decade: a visual medium.

A severed head of an elk, the bar's inspiration, its marble eyes dulled, its fur patchy and antlers obscene, stares down from above at the end of the narrow hallway to the bathrooms. Antlers is decidedly male and unaccustomed to such a throng of females or the waft of estrogen rising like mist—its makeshift stage not a stage, exactly, more a dais of the kind found for elevating politicians above a crowd.

Look now at Beth as she takes another bow! All the colleagues reluctant to let her go as she waves goodbye to the left, goodbye to the right, spoons still in hand though blouse fortunately buttoned up. Groups of women, some strangers, offer high fives as she threads through the tables. Constance watches then turns to Beth's quinoa, a hearty, fiberesque gray. She pictures opening her mouth and blowing, setting the entire place to flame or at least reheating the quinoa—she could do it, too, given what she's put down in the course of the last hour, given her general mood. A little fire would put a swift end to Storytelling Wednesdays.

We're all about inhibition, Mary Ann, the MC, recently tenured and flush from the publication of a bestselling dystopian novel, announced at the start of the evening, losing it, or possibly creativity, gaining it, reclaiming it, owning it, she had added. Her own story, kicking things off, had to do with her firstborn, a cesarean section, the doctor's hands deep in her gut, a recurring feeling even after he'd sewn her up, even after her newborn was a toddler, those hands still there, rooting around.

"Amazing!" Constance says to Beth, who slides, with a ginger handoff from Mary Ann, back into her seat.

"You liked?" Beth says.

"Loved. Completely loved. Insane. How did you even do that?"

"Practice," Beth says. "Muscle memory. Tim thinks it's a hoot."

Beth held two familiar-looking spoons in her hand.

"Your quinoa's cold," Constance says.

"I know," Beth says, scooping, chewing. "It's supposed to be. Well not cold, exactly, but not hot. Hot is too much. Lukewarm is best."

"I completely agree," Constance says.

Another mother story, not that anyone's asking: a day long ago, summer of '74 or thereabouts, Constance scrounging for spare change and possibly a cigarette in one of the cloisonné boxes in the living room. Constance is a teenager in tennis whites, a big match that afternoon. The living room is a room she rarely enters, sanctioned as it is for weekend gatherings of adults. They come in pairs like monogamous swans, arriving for her parents' famous cocktail parties, chitchatting among the heavy walnut furniture, the coffee table with its twisted, vined legs, the drawers of the tiger oak sideboard stuffed with silver she and her younger sister, Sally, polish with rags from the pantry the day before Thanksgiving, or Christmas Eve. On the walls are the artifacts from her parents' collections, her mother's framed Hans Christian Andersen illustrations, torn from an ancient valuable edition, a flea market steal: the Little Match Girl, shivering, and a near-dead Hansel and Gretel. And splayed on the living room couch, one arm across her eyes as if against a glare, her mother out cold.

Know Constance has come into fourteen like Juliet Capulet, lovesick, desperate, a pawn in the vagaries of jousting boys. She keeps a diary under lock and key and rarely tells anyone her true thoughts—how she alone can see the way the world tilts and slips off its axis, the way no one knows a thing but her. She understands in her bones that she will reinvent the universe in the image of something better, something as of yet unimaginable but just beyond the horizon of this failing world just as soon as she gets out. Now she loops her mother's arm over her shoulder and drags her up the stairs.

Soon the bridge group will arrive, clustering in the foyer—bags and shoes, curious expressions. They are here for their weekly game, they tell Constance, who has answered the door. They were on for 11:00, they say, and isn't that her mother's car still in the drive?

Who knew? Who didn't? Constance's mother had once not been far from the rest of them, if measured by this and that, yardsticks or swizzle, and now she'd soared straight into space: shot to the moon, tucked in bed where Constance has lugged her.

"Mother's upstairs," she says. "She's under the weather."

"It's going around," says Margaret Jones.

"I believe she knew we were coming," Florence Spears says.

"I told her I'd play her hand," Constance says, improvising. "I'm not bad. I've been teaching myself."

"She's been teaching herself," says Taffy Bott, as if Constance speaks French, and she must translate for the rest of them.

Constance smiles and holds up the cards, tall in her tennis whites, her legs and arms tanned. She explains they could play a rubber, maybe two, but she has a match in an hour and will have to cut it short.

She has her mother's eyes—they'd never noticed!—and a way of looking as if she might rip their throats. No doubt she has a killer serve.

Sally appears to offer lemonade, ten cents a glass.

"All right," they say. "If you're sure," they say. Everything almost fine and what isn't could be ignored: Constance subbing for her mother! Little Sally selling the lemonade! Eleanor Spears tells a funny story. Taffy Bott shows them her broken toe, the bruise reaching all the way to her calf. Margaret Jones has a summer cold but who doesn't?

Constance sets up the card table in the middle of the living room, the folding one from the garage still sticky with the spills from Sally's stand the weekend before. She sends Sally for a

113

tablecloth from the kitchen, cocktail napkins, a can of peanuts from the pantry.

The women eat the nuts in fistfuls, down their drinks quick. The cocktail napkins read, OF ALL THE THINGS I'VE LOVED AND LOST I MISS MY MIND THE MOST.

Beth walks Constance to her apartment, one of the nondescript new condos on Sheridan near the university. They burrow against the wind in their puffy, ugly coats, too cold to speak until the shelter of the courtyard.

"Would you like a nightcap?" Constance asks her.

"I've got midterms," Beth says.

"Right," Constance says. "Forgot," she says. Sabbatical haze, she says, her explanation, these days, for everything.

"Well, good night," Constance says, pulling open the heavy outer door to the vestibule. "You were great," she calls to Beth as the door slowly closes behind her. Within the vestibule there are the usual take-out menus and free newspapers scattered on the tiled floor, and someone has once again plastered the buzzer panel with stickers advertising a locksmith. CALL PHIL, the sticker reads, again and again. There must be a hundred of them, or hundreds. Phil everywhere. Constance reaches into her pocket for her key: a single key, unadorned. She likes it that way, though her ex-husband, Luke, is convinced she's a fool. You're a fool! Luke tells her every time she pulls her single, silver key out of her pocket. A fool!

But there's no key, only a piece of paper. A list. Folded over and over again as if top secret, the ink faded though clearly her mother's hand: To Do, it reads: bleach; *yarn;* Q-tips?; blueberries?; call Constance; organize girls; talk to William.

"What did I miss?" her mother wanted to know. She lay in bed eating the buttered toast Constance delivered on a tray. There were smells here beyond the homey toast, her mother's smells, and the cold smell of the big black telephone next to the bed where her mother and father slept, lying straight and still, side by side. Her mother's clothes were lined in the closet like so many other mothers and in the third drawer, behind the box with her mother's rings and pearls, the bottle of gin Constance had found foraging for cigarettes weeks earlier. She had swigged some for good measure, then poured the rest of it down the drain in her mother's master bathroom, the counter cluttered with her mother's makeup and perfumes, the mirror smudged in places, as if her mother had pressed her face to the glass.

"Nothing," Constance says. She has played her match, returning straight home along the road to the club. Somewhere between here and there she saw a flattened armadillo, its splintered shell streaked with brown blood. Someone must have dragged it to the dirt. She stinks of sweat dried to salt: if you licked her you could survive for a while but not forever. She has won her match in straight sets. In fact, the few onlookers, other girls' mothers, said they had never seen Constance serve so well: Constance playing as if her life depended on it. Her opponent, a taller, older girl named Macy Levitt, her glasses hooked with a needlepoint band, thought at first that Constance wasn't Constance at all, that somehow, in the time between now and before, Constance was replaced with a different Constance, not the Constance Macy Levitt knew from the past but a Constance from some distant, Amazonian tribe.

"So, you're the famous Phil," Constance says. He's arrived as promised, pulling up in his big tow truck as if this were the country, leaving it to idle, its headlights illuminating the two of them, casting their shadows backward out the glass door into the frozen courtyard, the withered rhododendron.

"Yes, ma'am," Phil says, pulling out a ring of keys, a bowling ball of keys.

"Good to meet you," she says.

"Same," he says.

Phil is stunningly handsome. She wouldn't have predicted it at all, but the world turns in

116

mysterious ways, as her mother would have said. Her mother would also have said, "There but for the grace of God go I"; "Hindsight is twenty-twenty"; and "Better than canned beer."

"Ma'am?" he says. She's been drifting, apparently. Sabbatical haze.

"Yes?"

"Done," he says, and she resists, as she's inclined to do, correcting his grammar. A turkey is done, she might say to him. You are *finished*.

"Really? Wow. I mean, I wasn't exactly watching, but that was fast."

"Yes, ma'am."

"I'm glad you left your stickers all over the place."

"Yes, ma'am."

The *ma'am* might have been irritating but the rest of him she liked. She remembers the story of her friend from college, who had invited the UPS guy in—this was a novelty back then, a man in a brown and yellow uniform on your doorstep, ringing your doorbell, goodies in large cardboard boxes in tow.

"How about a drink?" she asks Phil. "Would you like a drink? A nightcap? I was just going up and, boy, you really saved my life. No one answered the buzzer. The whole world is out. I mean, I have a cat and my son, well, he's with his father, but my son would have totally freaked if I couldn't get in to feed the cat. It's his cat."

"Sure."

"What?"

"Sure. I'll have a drink," Phil says. "I've got coverage."

"Coverage. Great!"

Phil holds the vestibule door open for her and then follows Constance into the elevator to her floor, brightly lit, a line of doors on either side, strangers within. It's Chicago real estate of a certain kind—thin walls, thin-glassed windows that leak heat in winter, the radiators blasting like nobody's business. Here the Little Match Girl looks entirely out of place—Constance has kept the print through college and graduate school, its twin, Hansel and Gretel, lost to a moldy basement in Oakland, unrecoverable.

It is very late when Constance finds herself naked from the waist up, attempting to balance spoons on her nipples—something we used to do at football parties, she lies—for the entertainment of the locksmith Phil, a man to whom she has already recited her mother's to-do list, hoping for a better reaction than the silence of Storytelling Wednesday. Phil had come through; he had applauded heartily.

"You get it?" she said. "You get it!"

They have finished the bottle she found in the refrigerator, their sex vigorous, inspired, or what she remembers of it, the couch wide enough for both of them though she preferred the floor.

Now he watches the spoons, which she has, after several attempts—muscle memory, she said—finally mastered. They balance from her nipples like silver icicles.

"Neat trick," Phil says, buttoning up. "I'll teach my wife."

Constance could eat Macy Levitt for lunch; she could pummel her with aces, lunge the net, drive the ball down her throat. She pictures it clearly. Think like a winner, her coach is saying, her coach a woman whose name has been engraved countless times in the trophies in glass outside the ladies' lounge: BABY ROLLINS, 1ST PLACE, LADIES SINGLES; BABY ROLLINS, 1ST PLACE, CLUB CHAMPIONSHIP; BABY ROLLINS & BEV WHITE, FIRST PLACE, et cetera, et cetera.

She beats Macy Levitt in straight sets; she makes Macy Levitt cry; she makes Macy Levitt throw off her glasses and stomp them with her Tretorns, losing the needlepoint band in the crabgrass next to the court, its fine handiwork sucked up and spit out shredded by the power mower a few days later, its driver entirely oblivious; she makes Macy Levitt drop out of the junior varsity team and years later, when she learns that Macy Levitt has been hospitalized for anorexia, she wonders if she also made Macy Levitt do that.

119

Constance reheats the coffee. She shuffles the stack of business cards Phil has left behind— what's with this guy?

Outside a bright moon and far below the scurry of late-night students, home from the library, the clubs, other dorm rooms elsewhere: the university taking over this neighborhood, once a place of revolutionaries and poets, men and women who labored in the slaughterhouses, whose fathers and mothers escaped lives so unspeakable they never spoke of them, their languages, their etymologies, submerged in the rising tide of English, their customs obliterated, or at least that's what the public said when the public weighed in, person after person waiting for her chance at the microphone.

But no one listened.

And here's another mother story, the part Constance doesn't like to tell: the reason for all this mother business. Why her mother is here again, as she will always be here again; Vassar girl, Katie Gibbs girl, a ghost perched on the narrow, faux-brass railing of the balcony only good for the cat litter and the trash she is too lazy to take down, a ghost stepping out of Hansel and Gretel, shaking the dead leaves from her sweater, still confused as to what path she was meant to follow: her smile, her crooked front tooth; or maybe standing on the corner with her last match.

"What'd I miss? her mother says, first complimenting Constance on her presentation—Constance has folded a linen napkin, one of her mother's favorite floral ones, next to the plate and sliced some bananas into a bowl. She has poured a glass of milk and picked a daylily from the long drive, put the flower in a silver bud vase. She wants everything nice.

But as she watches her mother's hand shake holding the toast, a feeling of pity or, rather, revulsion reaches up to tighten its hold, to grip her throat. It's a feeling Constance knows from catching her mother alone in padded bra and girdle, her mother's blue-white skin, the frayed straps of her complicated undergarments she has seen drying in the master bathroom, slung over the silver shower rod. So Constance does not say *nothing* as she sometimes remembers, cruel, cruel child that she was, that she continued to be; instead she waits, fingering the grass stain on her tennis skirt, a smudge of dirt on her wrist, her animal smell rank, furious.

"Everything," is what she says, looking back at her mother, whose green eyes, rimmed in red, stare out so hungry.

"You missed it all," she says.

PARIS, 1994

Into the City of Light she descends in darkness. Or this is how Rebecca hears it; I descend on the City of Light in darkness—a gray storm-ridden sky, clouds bunched in fat grape colors, a strange mauve. The city of stone streaked with pigeon shit, ripped rock-and-roll posters. A poet's place.

Rebecca cannot see but imagines the inside of all the passing storefronts: cafés, restaurants, boutiques where she has heard they arrange clothing by color.

Crowds on narrow sidewalks herd beneath umbrellas, everyone wearing a smart raincoat. Parisians. She is sure they are being taken for a ride.

"Did you ask him?" she asks Tom. "Does he know where to go?"

"He knows," Tom says, his eyes closed, head against the back of the cab seat. She turns away to the window. Paris, she thinks. The name enough. Round as a bun, the P. Marie Antoinette. The South; something about cake. Tanks barreling through the Arc de Triomphe. Springtime. Poplar blossoms. Or maybe, winter. She can't remember. She studied French once, in a classroom in a school whose name she has since forgotten, with a teacher who wore red wool dresses and clunky shoes. Mademoiselle, they called her. The boys with CB radios; the girls in cheerleading uniforms: Mademoiselle, they said, blowing smoke rings. *Merde*, they said in the hallways, it's time for French.

"I'm hungry," Rebecca says out the window, though she hears Tom's light snoring. The taxi moves slowly over a bridge and in the instant before it bumps onto the narrow street of their hotel, she glimpses a long gray river and silver domes of unimaginable heights.

Tom wakes from his nap and stretches his arms, touching walls on either side wallpapered a faded whorehouse red. Cracks in the plaster thin as hairs. The pillows smell of spiderwebs and sweet perfume. Rebecca opens the shutters then the glass doors of the window. Dust on her fingers, a tangerine glint to the rain. Orange light reflected in tiny tears; what had she heard? That insects fly through a downpour without getting wet. No insects here. No screens. Only flowerpots and wrought iron and four-story buildings painted the pastels of teacups and women with black hair and a constant din: a crowd far away pushing at the seams of quiet. Someone nearby coughs. Spits. Rebecca leans farther out the window. "You can see the gate to the Place des Vosges," she says, bending at the waist. She wears panties and a bra, her white skin mottled pink from cold, from rain.

She sits back down on the corner of the tiny bed and puts on her stockings.

"Who told you about this place?" Tom says.

"I read it," Rebecca says. She checks her stockings for runs, spreads a leg over five fingers, hand webbed black. "They said it was in the heart of the romantic district. Look," she says, "quack quack."

They walk in the rain; there is nothing else to do. She would like to tell him certain things, what she has done in the past or would like to do next, but every time she opens her mouth to speak she feels tired and stops. She had always thought to be in Paris with a husband meant to be bent, head to head, in discussion.

They wear long underwear, coats, and sweaters; Tom unshaven. Dark hair, face speckled with beard. She holds his hand. He holds an umbrella. She imagines them old; she imagines them closer to the ends of their lives. We are already old, she thinks.

They walk up the flat gray steps leading into the Bibliothèque Nationale and the galleries. In a dark and crowded room are the illuminated manuscripts they have heard about. Boxed in plastic. Yellow as jellyfish. Glowing. Devils swoon on every page: sharp-eared men with pointy noses, tiny fingernails, hovering on the shoulders of gentlewomen, knights, whispering Latin curses;

the colors—dyes pounded from berries and bark—bleed from other centuries' rainstorms, floods, natural disasters, Rebecca reads. People in raincoats push at her, stepping close to the plastic boxes, their collective breath hot.

Outside the rain has stopped. Clouds blow against the sun, people like swimmers underwater, dappled, squinting, slow moving. Rebecca and Tom join the tide, pushing along the sidewalk looking for a café that looks romantic. On the street they talk of their baby, how their baby could not help but be conceived in a city like this; what baby wouldn't want parents who roamed the world?

"Do you think they really choose?" Rebecca asks.

"What do you mean?" Tom says.

"Babies. You've heard that before. I've told you that before. That there's some theory that the baby chooses its parents, decides who it wants to be born to, who it likes."

He looks at her. She shrugs. "It makes sense," she says.

"You would have chosen Marion for a mother?"

"What did I know?" she says. "I wasn't even born."

A waitress leads them to a table in the back near four old men playing cards, a cane propped against the wall, mustard yellow, fissured. "Look," Rebecca says, pointing at them. "It's like we're in a painting."

She orders goat cheese and arugula, a glass of red wine. Tom orders oysters. To get him in the mood, he says. They sit with their hands entwined; they have nothing to say.

"Oh dear," Rebecca says, turning her face away from him to look out the big glass windows. "The City of Light's gone dark."

They came to Paris impromptu; this is how Rebecca would tell it. In truth, they look for a way of being together. Lately Rebecca, grown taller than Marion and with thin, gray streaks in her hair, has begun to resemble her father, Robert: his distance, his laugh. She feels distracted always, often alone; she would like to run through a rainstorm, or hunt big game somewhere. Marion has been dead a few months, her death quick and cruel, the cancer undetected, her organs gone spongy and blue. Rebecca often sees her. In doorways. Crossing the street. She is like all the women whose lives have given out on them too suddenly.

In response, Rebecca recently swore to live in the moment. No regrets; no sorrow. Only the next day and the next.

This decision happened near dusk on a regular weekend in the town where Rebecca and Tom now live, one road dividing their house from the Atlantic Ocean. From the living room, Rebecca often looked out the plate-glass window at an endless view and thought of nothing. She was doing just that when Tom walked in, cold from raking leaves, his hands gloved in pigskin, his boots muddy. He took off his gloves and his cold hands touched her face, her lips; she could smell dead leaves in his hair. When she lived in the city, in the studio apartment in the neighborhood that now seems to her intolerably dangerous, ridiculously so, she always thought, on Sunday afternoons, how she would like to smell the smell of dead leaves raked or burning, how she would like to step outside to an ocean.

Be careful what you wish for, she thought.

Tom pulled her down to the rag rug Marion had given to her as a housewarming present; he pulled her sweater over her head, his cold hands on her breasts. Perhaps it was the cold, or the smell of the leaves; perhaps she had been thinking about Marion's life after all.

She stood up and walked to their bedroom closet, to the drawer where she kept her diaphragm, its hard plastic case the color of a prosthesis. Normally, she would have crouched down on the closet floor to insert it, then rejoined Tom on the living room floor. But this time she carried it out to him, ceremoniously, first finding a pair of scissors in the kitchen.

"Are you watching closely?" she said. "This is a moment. This is the new me."

"Are you sure?" Tom said.

"No, but why not?" she said, sitting down and cutting the diaphragm in half. She held up the two pieces of the diaphragm as if debating. Then she carried the two halves into the kitchen to the trash. Tom wrapped his sweater around his waist and followed her.

"We should talk about this," he said.

She dumped the severed diaphragm in and sat down at the kitchen table, her breasts round, heavy, nipples brown.

"We should talk," he said again.

"We have," she said. "Anyway, there's no good time, really, is there? I mean, you either do it or you don't. And we know we don't want to don't, so we might as well do, right?"

"But are you sure?" he said, feeling a thrill saying it, as if to hear her say the word *yes* would somehow deliver her to him, her husband.

"This is a ridiculous conversation," she said. "Let's just fuck."

"Look at this," Rebecca says, showing Tom the postcard of devils she purchased earlier in the Bibliothèque gift shop. "Marion would have loved this. I could have sent it with a note, 'Having a devilish good time.' She'd think we were running nude in fountains or something."

Tom takes the postcard, pushing his eyeglasses down his nose to see clearly.

This is who we'll be old, Rebecca thinks. We'll think, We had a devilish good time, didn't we? She thinks of Marion and Robert traveling to New Zealand, returning to paste photographs in one of the albums they received each year for Christmas. We had a devilish good time, they would say.

She finishes her wine. Behind her the men at the card table argue, their voices raised. They smell of wet wool and cigarettes, hours spent over yellowing cards.

"It reminded me of something, of some poem I remember reading in school. A Blake one, I'm sure. Isn't he the one with the devils?"

"I thought he was the one with the chimney sweeps," Tom says.

"Maybe, there was something about visions and devils, I thought." She shrugs. "Anyway, I liked it. Marion would have thought it very cosmopolitan."

Rebecca picks at her wool pants. She is a little drunk, and suddenly the dusk seems to sweep her under a current of melancholy. She could cut off her ear and send it to someone, but whom? Melancholy, she thinks. Melancholia. The word mellifluous, exactly right. She thinks of a line she heard attributed to Van Gogh. Something about empty chairs, what was it? *Empty chairs—there are many of them, there will be even more.*

"Poor Marion," she says. "Poor baby."

· · ·

At night, Tom lies on the bed, his feet hanging over the edge of the soft mattress, his arms stretched above his head, palms turned and flat against the wall.

Rebecca walks across the tiny room, away from him, to the window. In the dark she can see across the street into another room; there a black-haired woman lights candles, bending over a table holding a long match. Red geraniums in clay pots, cobalt-blue shutters. It is as if Rebecca sees into a shadow box: a kitchen leading into a living room leading into a dining room. The black-haired woman straightens, pausing as if to admire the look of the table with light, then she steps away from the table and walks toward the door. Goodbye, Marion, Rebecca thinks.

"Let's go," she says, turning back to Tom. He lies on the bed. Long thin legs the most of him. Elbows. Neck. Large hands holding a guide to Paris. He wears his sneakers. White athletic socks pulled high, almost to his hairy knees.

"Now? It's late," he says.

"The Parisians are just sitting down to dinner. All across the city the Parisians are sitting down to dinner. Haven't you ever heard the expression *when in Rome?* For Chrissakes."

She turns away from him, back to the window. The shutters have been drawn closed, though there is still light in the rooms; she imagines the woman coming in from the kitchen now with some sort of cognac. And pears. There would be ripe yellow pears, sliced with pearly-handled silver. Heirlooms passed down in worn wooden chests, kept in corners covered in maroon velvet; everything draped with a soft worn fabric documenting a certain tenable history. The woman would bend close to the frame as she set down the plate, wooden, that held the yellow pears, and the light might catch the sheen in her black hair, brushed hard every evening the way she had been taught by her mother, who learned from her mother. And so on.

There would also be cheese.

"I don't know. I want some cognac, or a plate of fruit and cheese. Wouldn't that be nice? To just, on a whim, go out close to midnight for a plate of fruit and cheese? For a cognac?"

Tom swings his long legs off the bed. "Sure," he says.

"What will we name it?" Rebecca asks him in the morning. They sit in a café across from Saint-Sulpice, waiting for the church to open; somewhere bells ring, and when the trucks go by, the pigeons that roost on the backs of the gargoyles erupt, their wings white and gray-speckled. Rebecca has read that the guard who lives across the street grows tomatoes on his roof and in the summertime hands them out to tourists.

Tom looks up from the *Herald Tribune*, a mustache of milk foam above his lip. "The baby?" he says.

"Of course," she says.

"I don't know," he says, looking back down. "That's bad luck."

"Why?"

"We haven't even, you know. I mean it could take a year; it could never happen at all."

He pretends to read; she knows better.

"Hello? Hello, monsieur. I'm talking to you."

"I don't like these games."

She feels rebuked, a child. She looks down at the black wool skirt she has put on; when they were in Istanbul, she wore long skirts the books said were required, even though the German tourists were practically nude. Here, she feels dowdy; the Parisian women so composed. She wants to buy yards of fabric and sew curtains for every window of their home. Yards and yards of tulle, or stiff silk, brilliant yellows and blues. She sees herself sewing, bent over into the night; in the morning she buys armloads of tulips and bleaches the floor white. If anyone asks why we've done it this way you can tell them it was my idea, she tells Tom. All my idea.

"Mademoiselle?" Tom says.

She looks up. He has wiped his mouth; the beard he grows on vacations, stiff. A handsome man, she thinks. I have married a handsome man.

"How about Sophie?" he says.

"Sophie? I never would have thought of that."

He shrugs and looks back down at the paper. "I always liked that name," he says.

"We could put Marion somewhere, too. Sophie Marion. Oh, God, that's awful."

"Marion?" Tom looks at her. "Really?"

"I don't know," Rebecca says. She picks at the wool. "Yes. I think I should honor her somehow. Give her something of me." Rebecca can't decide whether she feels dramatic or bored, whether she is at all sure of these words, or whether she is simply trying to distract Tom from his newspaper.

"There are a lot of regrets," she says. "A lot of things I might have done differently. I might have talked to her about. She couldn't help it. The way she was. She was of a certain time. And then I think, I'm like her. And I'm terrified of that, of course. But I'm not sure why. She was a decent woman, wasn't she? Now I can't even remember the last thing I said to her."

"It had something to do with the television."

"What do you mean?"

"I remember. We were in her hospital room. Something about whether she wanted the television—"

"Shut up," Rebecca says, feeling foolish. "I don't mean like that. I mean, the last thing I *said* to her."

They enter Saint-Sulpice with a few other tourists, a boy with long hair and a guitar case strapped to his back, two elderly women. "It says that this brass meridian line," Tom reads to Rebecca, "represents France's eighteenth-century passion for science."

Rebecca steps on France's passion for science, following Tom toward the altar; he turns to examine a rosette and she continues to the famous portrait of the Virgin and Child she has read about; the child's face looks like an old man, as if he weren't born a baby but someone who had already lived a life, made up his mind; the Virgin's face looks like a baby's face.

In front of the portrait, long thin white candles burn in a candelabra; what looks like a parking meter has been mounted in front of the candelabra. For three francs, the sign reads in English, anyone can buy another candle to light. The money will be sent to a missionary in Bhutan.

Rebecca counts out her coins and puts them into the meter; then she holds the long thin candle against one of the many flames.

"Poor Marion," she says. "Poor Sophie."

When Rebecca first met Tom, she lived in her studio apartment and he lived in California, in a rented house with white stucco walls and a fireplace he never used. When they could, they would spend evenings sitting on the couch in her studio, looking out the window to the park across the street, to the trees and swing set. The lights made the shadows grow to other things.

She could have lived in Florence with a man named Mohammed, she told him, or been in the movies with the owner of the place where she stayed in Jamaica; she could have met someone in Rajasthan and ridden elephants. Or lived on the island in Greece where the old widow ran her television on a car battery. The widow's room faced the Aegean Sea. Each morning the old woman cooked her an omelet of fresh eggs and goat cheese, browned at the edges, and she would sit beneath grapevines looking out to the Aegean Sea, at a wooden table carved with the initials of summer tourists who had come to stay.

Tom said he could have been a passenger on the train that crossed Canada, but they had canceled the route before his departure date.

Despite this, she fell in love with him, first falling in love with his name: Tom, a big *T* and a little *o* and an *m*. Sounded good in her mouth when she said it: I'll be dining with Tom this evening. Tom and I are going out. Tom thinks. Tom Tom Tom Tom Tom. Tom was in a difficult relationship. Tom had a bad time of it. Tom will be in on Thursday.

People liked Tom. Marion and Robert. They

liked his big hands and his little glasses and the way he would play the guitar at parties and the way he always sang a song he wrote at college. No one really understood the words but they found it quaint.

When she traveled to California, to his town, they would wake up early and hike down to the dock on the water where the boat owners came for eggs and sit at the picnic tables watching the seagulls land so close the tourists would duck, and Tom would pull apart soggy bread and throw it up for the seagulls so they would catch it in their gray beaks. This and a cigarette shared from time to time, a single bought from the drugstore to be smoked on the cliffs overlooking the Pacific, the sound of the roller coaster as constant as the surf, were the elements of their courtship.

But there seemed a certain adventure in what they had then; they look to resume it in Paris, though both feel awkward here, as if they are watched from every window, their actions exaggerated, their voices loud and shrill, their feet too big and hands too big and minor imperfections of skin large and ugly. They hadn't expected such cold, and now they must bundle up in bulky awkward coats, their legs and arms constricted by underwear; wool hats hide their faces as they walk, glove in glove, down the Champs-Élysées, aware of the cold in their feet and their runny noses and the bare trees.

. . .

Rebecca does not look at Tom's face over her. She can feel him sometimes, his prickly cheek, chin. She tries to think of other things than babies, but they float out to her on clouds, cherubs pink as the angels in the illuminated manuscripts. She remembers a friend saying that making love pregnant was like having someone watching; she feels this already, a soul hovering, debating whether to come back into this world.

Now, Tom sleeps as she listens to the knocking radiator, the hiss of steam.

She pulls her nightgown from beside the bed and puts it on. Across the street the room with the black-haired woman looks empty; tulips in a glass vase, pears ripening on the wooden plate. She is cold and gets back in bed. I've been thinking, she whispers, though Tom is lightly snoring. Maybe I don't want to do this after all.

At dinner Tom orders champagne, more oysters; the restaurant, cavernous, dark, swelling with the voices of a hundred Frenchmen; some sort of argument seems to have erupted at every table. "What is everyone saying?" Rebecca asks. "Something seems to be going on."

"Wine, I think," Tom says. "Wine and good food." He seems entirely pleased. He has put on a jacket and a pressed shirt, buttoning the cuffs. His beard looks planned, cultivated, no longer the result of days unattended. His glasses are bright and clean. At times she finds herself staring at him as if he is entirely unfamiliar to her, a blind date or somebody's cousin she has agreed to meet. "What are you thinking?" he says.

"Marion," she says. "I was thinking of how she always spoke of coming to Paris and now here I am." Rebecca looks around her; on the brick wall is a framed print she recognizes: still life with fruit.

"I'm trying to imagine her in Paris, actually, and for some reason I can't get a kelly green coat out of my mind. I think she would have worn a kelly green coat, whatever that is, and some sort of smart hat, and I think she would have come to the city in warm weather, and would have sat in the cafés and watched the people and met some dashing Frenchman named Monsieur something who wouldn't have minded her at all."

Tom gestures to the waitress for the check, his pinkie extended as he signs his name in the air. Rebecca looks away, down at her brown wool pants.

"Sounds like Audrey Hepburn in *Gigi*," he says. "Marion would have hated the food."

In the middle of the night Rebecca wakes to screaming, or wailing, really, something wounded, in pain. Descendants of a revolution she has never completely understood, though she knows that it lasted forever and continues, that there has been some terrible violence.

Tom snores, a washcloth over his eyes to keep the light from the street out; she has insisted on leaving the shutters open, the window open. Tom is out like a light in the City of Light, she thinks. Tom, my husband. My husband, Tom. His father, Tom. Her father, Tom. That's the boy's father, Tom. His grandmother, Marion, is dead.

She sits up, gets out of bed and walks to the window to see; outside, the cobblestones glisten with rainwater; it is the time of night impossible to know: she may have been sleeping an hour, it may be almost dawn.

She will tell him tomorrow. What, she isn't sure, but something, surely. I am bored, she will say, or I love you, madly. Let's divorce. Let's not. Let's go on. Let's stop.

Across the street, the black-haired woman sits in a circle of light, fresh tulips in a vase beside her; she wears pajamas that look like men's pajamas, pants and a tunic; she has crossed her legs and Rebecca can see one thin ankle, milk white, hanging just below the hem.

Rebecca looks away. There is something too perfect about it, the scene. It is what they all wanted, isn't it? Marion. Rebecca. Sophie. The something someone else had; the life seen through a frame: to be a black-haired woman, to eat a ripe pear.

Beneath the window the cobblestones shine wet. She might hear horse hooves, the quiet clopping of a team on their way to the Place des Vosges. She tries to see but the street is empty, shops shuttered and dark, water pooled in places, a cat. Into this she imagines the carriage, a woman behind its shuttered windows on her way somewhere else, her hand gloved in white velvet, her body swathed in stiff silk: a princess, a saint, a mother, a daughter, a goddess borne out of this place to another: a palace, an attic. There are babies there and devils, too; they are all of them hovering there waiting to descend, waiting to be asked, waiting to choose, waiting for their chance to be born.

A MOTHER IS SOMEONE WHO TELLS JOKES

Helen walks late into the salon, Lucy on another client: what looks like a low light. Lucy pauses, her hands in blue surgeon's gloves. "Did you see? Did you come Twenty-third?" she asks, waiting.

The other client waits, too, framed in Lucy's baronial mirror or, at the very least, Baroque: the vanity, not the other client; the other client is decidedly Modern, Frank Lloyd Wright or Louis Kahn, glass and steel, angular, with perfect acoustics and a smart bag. "It was incredible," she says, a smudge of black dye on her forehead, hair foiled and epic. "Amazing."

"What?" Helen says. "What are we talking about?"

"No one knows," Lucy says. She secures the last tinfoil fold then peels off her gloves. "They were in the sky."

"On Twenty-third," the other client says. "Twenty-third and Eighth," she says, her neck an alabaster column up from a black robe, her head a severed Medusa.

Big has been dreaming of a cataclysmic event and Helen is on her last nerve. Who wouldn't be? He wakes odd hours to report what's to come next and who's involved, sometimes teachers from Park Lane, his old school, and sometimes children with whom he has long lost touch— the grown boy from 5F they see buzzing in or hurrying out. In Big's dreams, Helen and Max escort survivors onto boats or pieces of driftwood, sweep broken glass into dustbins. Helen rips their good sheets for tourniquets. It's nice to know I'm handy in an emergency, Helen says, smoothing Big's hair as she tries to balance next to him on his narrow twin bed, too small for Big but still he insists, preferring to scrunch tight against the plastic guardrail as he sleeps or doesn't sleep.

"You'd think I would faint," she says. "I mean, ripping my *good* sheets?"

"It's an emergency," Big says.

"That would take an emergency," Helen says.

"Shut *up,* Helen," Big says, kicking at his cowboy comforter, agitated, although usually he will laugh at her jokes: this is what Mrs. MacIntyre had said. Keep your sense of humor! Mrs. MacIntyre had said. Mrs. MacIntyre always their favorite, Big's nursery school teacher all those years back, of the MacIntyre and Farrell fame, she would say, raised in a circus in Narragansett-by-the-Sea, her first friend a chimpanzee—true story—named Charlie Darwin. It had all rhymed.

Big adored her. All the children adored her. How could they not adore her? She wore hats with plastic flowers. She owned kitten heels. "Here, kitty, kitty," she would say, slipping them on to walk the children down the stairs and down the street to one of the playgrounds in Riverside Park. She had promised if they were well behaved and kept quiet voices and still hands she would bring in the photo of Charlie Darwin from the highly regarded newspaper known as *The Boston Globe*. She had promised she would read to them from the article entitled "Inseparable" featuring a certain teacher they might recognize at a certain age close to their own. In the photograph, this certain teacher wore white cotillion gloves and satin shoes handed down to her by one of the Freaks whose feet had been bound in a place far away known as *China,* she said, where these things once happened and where life is very different from our own.

Is any of it true? Big wanted to know.

In the corner of her classroom, Mrs. MacIntyre kept a box turtle named Francis Galton and a bowl with Useless Information she read aloud before Nap. Francis Galton, the real Charles Darwin's cousin, Shakespeare born the year Michelangelo died. Tidbits that might come in handy, she told them, when carrying on a conversation. She had projects to construct, ideas to execute: before Mother's Day she asked the children to fill in the blank: A mother is someone who . . . She would write their words, she said, and they could illustrate. Together they would make a book.

Lily P. drew a set of stairs heading up to a bed, a circle on the bed with slashes for eyes and a crooked mouth. Beneath this Mrs. MacIntyre wrote: "A Mother Is Someone Who Takes Naps." Sebastian drew a circle with lines shooting out of it, like the sun. "A Mother Is Someone Who Crosses the Street," it read in Mrs. MacIntyre's neat cursive. That was interesting, Helen had told Big, reading, but Big's was best: "A Mother Is Someone Who Tells Jokes." Big's drawing a circle that took up the entire page, its center blank.

Helen strokes the stubble on Big's cheek. He needs to shave.

"A mother is someone who tells jokes," she says, willing Big to look at her and smile.

But Big isn't looking. He's staring off where he stares. "You don't *faint,* Helen," he says, his eyes wide in the half-dark, his cowboy quilt—too warm for this weather—at the footboard she found at Goodwill and painted all those years ago with scenes from Winnie-the-Pooh. "You get us out of trees."

"We're in the trees?"

"Tree*tops.*"

"In New York?"

"There are treetops, Helen. There are lots of treetops in New York."

"We're in a park?" she says. "That's nice." She pulls the quilt up to cover him. He is all arms and legs and hairy kneecaps.

"Helen?"

"Yes?"

"Do you like cats or dogs?"

Down the hall Max snores, oblivious. For many years Big was in their bed, and then, when Max insisted, Helen moved Big back to Big's room, although most nights here she is with him, sitting on the floor or leaning against the plastic guardrail. She had explained to Max that Big needed to know she was there when he closed his eyes and Big needed to know she was there when he opened his eyes. It is what it is, she said to him, her husband, a man who now moves through the apartment like a quiet boarder, someone from the nineteenth century with a whispered past and stockinged feet, unassuming, baffled by life's circumstances.

"Both," she says. "I like both," she says.

"I like cats. Slinky was our cat."

"Slinky was our cat."

"There were cats in the treetops but Slinky wasn't there."

"Wasn't he?" Helen says: Slinky the Cat, adopted from Bide-awee, a gray kitten, wide-eyed, terrified, its stubby, shaky legs, as if always a giraffe just up from a pose. Big had carried Slinky to the window to look out.

151

"Slinky was a funny cat," Big says.

"Yes," Helen says. "Slinky was a very funny cat."

She saw nothing on Twenty-third, Helen tells Lucy and the other client, who now broils in the corner beneath the red heat lamp, a woman's magazine in her lap. Lucy has fastened a black robe around Helen's neck and raised the chair so Helen sits squarely in the view of the baronial mirror, her face reflected in its fissured, antique glass as if a spectral vision, a ghost from history, a canvas you might dream of and then wake unsettled. Lucy has decorated the elaborate chandelier overhead as fits Lucy's cheerful character: white doves and sparkly fake snow, loops of low-hanging dime store pearls—careful, Lucy says, as Helen settles in. Wonderful, love, Lucy says, mixing Helen's formula. Helen watches as Lucy begins to paint the dye on the white line of her part, starker in the chandelier light than in her bathroom mirror at home, though in truth she rarely looks in that mirror: it's a good day if she gets to shower.

She had actually crossed Twenty-second, and been *delayed,* she tells them, by a small gathering around Starbucks commemorating Edith Wharton, who had lived there—not the *Starbucks,* of course, though, hah! think of that—Edith Wharton and Henry James ordering a grande macchiato with extra foam—no, the gathering had been to place a plaque on what had apparently once been Edith Wharton's home, or work space, or something, the gathering including an impromptu reading from Wharton's New York stories Helen had not recognized but felt she should.

Helen waits for Lucy or the other client to comment, but Lucy seems so absorbed in painting Helen's part that she may not have heard a word. She methodically dips the paintbrush into the little plastic bowl in her hand then lifts and coats a swath of hair, the cold dye burning Helen's scalp, the threads of thick cotton around her ears already itchy. The other client, God knows; Helen can no longer see her: she might be sizzled to a crisp. Broiled to nothing.

"I saw the *Pride and Prejudice* with whatshisname as Darcy," the other client suddenly says or, rather, yells: difficult to be heard within the helmet of heat.

"Colin Firth," Lucy says, tucking the cotton into the collar of Helen's robe; a trickle of dye wet on Helen's neck.

"Don't even," the other customer yells. "Colin Firth. *Young* Colin Firth."

"That's Austen," Helen yells back, a little pissed for reasons she can't name. "Jane Austen."

"I know," the other client yells. "That's what I said."

● ● ●

It was Mrs. MacIntyre who first used the word *spectrum,* a word that still brings to Helen's mind an arch of good-luck colors, a rainbow, Big sliding down like the goddess Iris to deliver an indecipherable message from Mount Olympus, his beautiful pale face scrunched with concentration. What you will learn, Mrs. MacIntyre had said, is that although *here* is not where you imagined you would be, there is beauty here nonetheless. You might have imagined you were taking a trip to Italy and had all sorts of ideas of what Italy would be, what you would do there, where you would go, the meals, the art, the warm people, and so forth, Mrs. MacIntyre had said.

Helen and Max sat across from her in tiny seats at a tiny table, Mrs. MacIntyre's voice naturally amplified as if the oracle at Delphi. Surrounding them were the many plush stuffed animals Mrs. MacIntyre refused to get rid of even after the lice epidemic, each stuffed animal named and adopted by one of the children, a special buddy they would find before morning meeting and hold in their laps as they sat in a circle on the circular carpet outlined with the alphabet.

"And then the door opens and, without warning, Antarctica!" Mrs. MacIntyre continued. "Not a place you ever imagined you would be, not even a place you wanted to visit. All you know of Antarctica is ice and cold."

"And penguins," Helen had said, because she could not stand it: she could not stand the way Mrs. MacIntyre was speaking to them, as if they, too, were sitting on the circular alphabet carpet, name tags pinned to their chests. First-day jitters. How did Mrs. MacIntyre know a goddamn thing? The woman was raised in a circus!

"I blame the city," Helen's sister-in-law later said. "Get out. Living there in those tiny spaces? It's like raising veal," she said, the two of them staring at her high-achieving suburban boys, pale as the moon, waxing, or possibly waning, poured like beams onto the couch in their basement rec room, deep into their video games.

But still, Antarctica. In the end it wasn't a bad way of describing everything, she supposed. Think of ice, she found herself saying to Big, trying to explain to him the fact of him after all the various experts and diagnoses, after he started asking questions. For example, she said, imagine if ice were denser than water, which you would think it would be, right? But if ice were denser than water, then a lake would freeze from the bottom up and life, what we know as the entire chemistry of life, would cease to exist.

"This is the point," she told him. "*Everything* is a mystery."

What did she even remember of Edith Wharton? The ones she had loved were the Romantics, and Wharton was unlike any of those women, the women among the Romantics, women who seemed to, at a moment's notice, drop their lives to sail to the continent with dying lovers, or tempestuous lovers, or lesbian lovers, towing their children behind or leaving their children behind or never having children at all. They changed their names and dressed like boys. They lived on nothing more than water and what they caught with their hands from the sea. Wharton, as she remembered, had been wealthy, a woman of society, or at least of means.

Not like Wordsworth's sister, Dorothy, galumphing next to her brother as he walked through daffodils, or so Helen imagined, Dorothy calling to him from the lakeshore as he rowed one way and then another, as he watched the shadows, the play of light, reveling in his spots of time. Or maybe Dorothy hadn't called to him from the lakeshore at all, maybe she had steered the boat. So many of the women did. Unnoticed. Quiet. Allowing the geniuses to concentrate and scribble. Scribblers, Smith called them; Smith himself, he let on, guilty of penning a sonnet or two. But alas his other tasks, namely education of overachieving midwesterners who couldn't give a damn, got in his way. She had adored him: greasy-haired, shy, the fifth Beatle or the reincarnation of one of her hero poets, a graduate student charged with this discussion group, their

TA. Then she had dried her hair straight and kept endless index cards with sentences written in her studied, loopy hand. Pens bought at the co-op for their colors, their promised clarity: green, purple, pink. Smith barely audible, mumbling and still— it was a terrible crush.

Plus, he smoked! His cigarette balanced in a glass ashtray he took out of his mailbag, stuffed with their papers he graded in his cramped hand, ellipses, she remembers, as if everything he wrote actually meant something more, something too overwhelming to articulate, too profound. First, always, he placed the ashtray on the wooden desk at the front of the room—those days when chairs still faced forward—and then slowly he took his rolling papers and bag of tobacco from his corduroy jacket, an olive green that nicely clashed with his khaki pants and tennis sneakers. He took a while, rolling the cigarette he would smoke as he recited his Wordsworth, his Byron, his Coleridge, his Shelley, at times pausing to pick tobacco from his tongue, or lip, the cigarette, almost gone, balanced against the sullied picture of Margaret Thatcher in the glass ashtray's well. He would eventually stub the butt on her face in rebellion. His teeth were predictably long and yellow, yet his eyes, as she remembers, were a glorious, stormy gray.

Lately, to keep awake, she recites "Tintern Abbey," her favorite, from the bookshelf in Big's room that still holds those textbooks, *Norton Anthology*'s index to the Romantics. She had forgotten. The Romantics were her favorites; the Romantics were always her favorites.

"Who were they?" Big asks.

"I don't know," she says. "People. They had amazing lives though short, too. They were always sailing to new places, beautiful places like Greece and Spain, but by the time they got there they had compromised lungs, things to worry about. It can happen. They also drowned a lot or, I mean, a bunch of them drowned."

Big worries his arm.

"Oh," he says.

He doesn't sleep so good, he'll tell you. His nights have become second days. Dark days. Morning the beginning of night, or sleep; eyes closed and dreaming, lightly, or is it deeply then? He has purple circles under his eyes; she has purple circles under her eyes. She sits on the side of his bed against the plastic guardrail but then she cannot; then she's too tired and simply has to go to sleep.

"I simply have to go to bed," she says.

"Who the fuck told you not to, Helen?" he says.

He's not mean that way. He might say *fuck off* but those are just words. He's gotten into trouble, he'll tell you, with his words, but he is a sweet boy, the sweetest boy. On the subway once he would not hold the pole and she insisted. She

158

insisted that he hold the pole, Big with no idea how big he was, how much he would hurt people if he knocked into the crowds and toppled anyone over and when she insisted he said, "Fuck you, Helen! Fuck you! Fuck you! Fuck you!"

The pages from the mother book were tacked all around the classroom. She moved from one to the next: circles within circles within circles. Every mother a circle: eyeless, many-eyed, small, large, but a circle nonetheless. "A Mother Is Someone Who Goes to Work," one read. Thomas A., his circle drawn with a thick, red crayon. It may have been a door, she supposed, or a window, or anything else to look through, to walk out of, to walk into: she thinks of Thomas A.'s mother, Dominique, a woman rarely seen, certainly not last week or the week before at the penny drive— all those pennies! Other mothers lugged bags of change they did not need to support something they were not entirely clear on: she wonders what Dominique thought when she read Thomas A.'s definition, whether she felt proud or horrified, whether she imagined all the unwritten lines above and beneath Mrs. MacIntyre's scrawl, or whether she moved on to Lily P.'s and laughed, thanking God at least not for that; she was not a mother who took naps.

"A Mother Is Someone Who Bakes Bread," Jose F.; "A Mother Is Someone Who Takes Too

Long," Stephanie D.; "A Mother Is Someone Who Drives a Car," Edith J. Helen studied each one as Max, folded into the tiny chair at the tiny table, listened to Mrs. MacIntyre and took notes.

Helen stands with the crowd on Twenty-third—hair so fresh, blown dry and dyed a mink brown, that in the midst of the crowd you might think she was someone you recognized from somewhere, a restaurant or a college reunion.

She stands with the rest of them arrested by the spectacle, shading her eyes to look up at the wonder of it: thousands of something that seem to have invaded the cloudless sky. She supposes they are unidentifiable; they are certainly other. Inexplicable though everyone wants to explain. To Helen they look like tiny, shimmering tears in the fabric of the blue sky. Poetic, she laughs. It is such a blue sky; such a remarkable day.

"I think they're amazing," a beautiful girl next to her says. Twenties or so, bracelets up her arm and other piercings. "They look kinda fishy, like a school of fish you see in the water, minnows, when the sun hits right," she says.

"What?" someone says.

"She thinks they look like fish," someone else says.

"Oh," the person says.

Helen does not want to move; no one does. What will happen next? Will these things land?

Explode? Continue to hover? She has stayed too late at Lucy's salon, lulled by Lucy's offer of tea, by the decorative chandelier, by Lucy's collection of coffee table books and her good cheer. Lucy had made her promise to return by way of Twenty-third, to see if what had been happening was still happening. But she has a grocery list in her pocket. At 5:00, the millionth babysitter she has found to watch Big in the afternoon will have to leave and she'll take over, helping Big practice his script, practice his math, practice his flute, practice his staring. They're working on it: they call it the Staring Olympics.

You're going to stare straight into my eyes for three minutes and then you're going to tell me exactly what color my eyes are, she's said. You're going for the gold, she's told him.

"Brown," he says.

"No, gold," she says.

"Your eyes are brown," he says.

"Right!" she says.

"You love dogs," he says. "You love dogs more than cats. You said it. You said you hated Slinky."

"Oh, Big," she says. "I loved Slinky. You know I loved Slinky. Slinky was the best cat ever."

"No, you love dogs more," he says. "You said it."

"I did," she says. "I wanted to make you feel better."

She touches his arm in the spot where it is okay

sometimes to touch him and still he flinches, as if he's been burned.

"Dogs or cats?" he says.

"You!" she says, staring, though he has already turned away.

"They're humming," an old lady says. "Listen, they're humming," she says, and the group surrounding them quiets down but there's no humming to be heard. "Never mind," the lady says. "Must have been me."

"You hum?" a man says. He's in a shiny business suit, the kind you buy at a closeout sale. He has already told everyone that he's missed the job interview anyway but he doesn't give a shit because there's no way in hell they'd hire him and he was only going because of his wife or his mother or his social worker or someone. He's jittery, possibly high, but he looks fresh and clean in his shiny suit and gives the whole gathering an air of legitimacy, Twenty-third and Eighth not known for its business suits.

"My grandmother used to do that," the beautiful girl says.

"What happened to her?" the old lady says.

"Oh, I don't know. She died," the girl says.

No one takes their eyes off the sky and the quivering slivers of light that may or may not be inhabited.

"I'm sorry," a few of them say at once.

162

"It's okay," the beautiful girl says. "I was, like, six or something."

Helen wonders how long she'll stand here, watching, not the beautiful girl—she will be here forever, and when she's gone, another will take her place—but her, Helen, promising student of Romantic poetry (the lark!), wife to Max, mother to Big. She should be on her way but also she should stick it out; to leave now would be to miss something important, she thinks, or worse: to never have been here at all.

The villagers run to the trees but they are fools because who is going to find them afterward? Big says. They will all be gone, bones washing up to shores of every continent and do they in these circumstances? He wants to know. He's been meaning to ask, he says, and she thinks, *circumstances,* and Big's so big.

But she says, I don't know, and thinks: It's 3:00 a.m.

"Anyway, you are and so is Max—" he says.

"Oh," she says.

"And you are in the highest trees and reaching down to me and trying to pull me up but I'm too big and it's getting higher—"

"What?"

"Are you fucking *deaf?* The water!" he says. "Sorry, Helen," he says.

"Are you wet, sweetheart?"

"Maybe," he says.

She gets up and says, "Please continue," as she strips Max's twin bed and puts the cowboy sheets in the bathtub to soak and wash in the morning. He says she can't hear him in the bathroom but she calls out I can, I can! and so he keeps talking and she returns with fresh sheets and makes the bed, checking the comforter for any wet spots and finding none tucking it in beneath the mattress and wedging it through the plastic guardrail and he is almost to the good part, he says, and she says, All right, all right, I'm listening, sweetheart. And she does. She sits on the edge of his twin bed and does; close up to the guardrail, she listens.

Smith was Reginald Smith, and though you'd think he'd ask to be called Reg, he did not. She stood at the door to his office, waiting, embroidered bell-bottoms and a cotton shirt bought along the boardwalk of the Jersey Shore; she also wore one of those shrinking hemp bracelets on her wrist, though she'd had half a mind to cut it off before school started and now, noticing, felt how childish it must look, the bracelet, how utterly ridiculous.

His jokes fell flat because they were not funny but she loved him for trying, and she loved him for everything. Professor Smith? she asked, and he said yes and invited her in and she sat in the chair across from his desk and he stood or

164

leaned over her to look at what she had written or what she was proposing to write, something about the letters between Dorothy and William Wordsworth, something about platonic ideals or some other hogwash, and Helen remembers and wants now to knock on the office door again, to interrupt this silly girl and this no doubt intelligent man to say, Don't bother. Or, Love her. Or, Take her with you. Or, something else she can't think what.

It is bright in the room. Certain nights Big can't have the lights out.

"So, what happened?" Big says. He is awake after all.

"Nothing," she says. "I just left."

Sometimes, when she is so tired, she tells Big everything.

At first she didn't see it. I'm not seeing anything, she said to the guy beside her. A guy is right beside her, and they are standing very close as strangers sometimes do in crowds. He is about her age but not her type but still she would like to lean on him, to put her head on his shoulder. Her scalp still burns. The dye has seeped into the gray roots—something about opened follicles—and covered the gray like so many shovels of dirt on a patch of bright white snow. But she knows the burning will pass.

"There," he says, pointing. She squints and

looks again. She might see something: squiggles. But they might be dust motes, or those things in your eye when you look straight at light.

She stares anyway, willing herself to see: the Staring Olympics.

She wants to be a person who sees, who believes in things, like Bigfoot, or God. She studies these persons and asks them lots of questions, which they happily answer before tiring of her—she can tell when people tire of her. So many questions! It's not that she wants to run them down, she just wants to understand—for instance, the Holy Ghost, she'll say. Who is he? Or is it He? Sometimes, in the middle of it, she won't be able to help herself—do you like cats or dogs?—she'll ask, just to hear. Most people who believe in things prefer dogs, she's told Big. It's true.

Mrs. MacIntyre had said she understood the shock of it but that she knew from children. Mrs. MacIntyre had said there was no doubt in her mind. Helen listened but then she did not: "A Mother Is Someone Who Doesn't Listen"; "A Mother Is Someone Who Makes It Up."

Nearby, on the bulletin board, Helen sees *The Boston Globe* article of the circus as promised. She stares at the photograph and feels a sharp burning behind her eyes she refuses to give in to: "A Mother Is Someone Who Does Not Give In to That Shit." The paper is aged. In the picture a little-girl Mrs. MacIntyre wears a white pinafore and what look like lace-up boots. She holds hands with her best friend, the chimpanzee Charlie Darwin. The chimpanzee towers over her, its eyes kind. They wear matching cotillion gloves. Behind them the big sign for MacIntyre & Farrell casts a shadow on the ground as a llama crosses in the background, oblivious.

When Helen returns from Lucy's, Big looks online for anything else he can learn of Helen's story, which sounds crazy to him, entirely unbelievable. But there they are! Scratchy images of slivers of light hovering over Twenty-third, schools of air minnows, flashing fish, captured by scores of handheld devices and already posted. Many in number, hundreds, possibly thousands, and looking, in any shot, like so many ctches of absence—as if someone has taken a pen and scratched at thc sky. Videos on YouTube show more of the same: flickers, hovering, a suggestion of something but, why? What? On the television, local news anchors do not quite know what to say: they speculate that this clear phenomenon might have to do with sun glancing off the wing of an ascending jet out of Newark, a kind of shattered prism effect, they say, similar to the phenomenon of heat mirages: the time the Taj Mahal hovered over the East River.

On NY1 they believe this might have to do with ongoing testing near the Hudson, testing of a confidential manner but nonetheless testing, as confirmed by the Twenty-second Precinct, which, when called, forwarded all inquiries to the Department of Homeland Security, causing a temporary overload and shutdown of the switchboard system that frankly, according to experts brought into NY1, is of far greater concern than a little inexplicable activity over Twenty-third Street.

"Well," Big says after hearing it. "It *is* true."

"I told you," Helen says. "No one knows. They have more theories than Heinz has beans."

"They're idiots!" Big yells. He watches the news with his arms wrapped around his hairy legs. He wears long gym shorts as if he has just been to basketball practice but he has not just been to basketball practice. He has been in his room eating Halloween candy, the floor littered with wrappers although she had expressly told the sitter to watch for that. Hadn't she said, expressly, to watch for that?

But this is much earlier and now she is tired and Big is tired and she thinks maybe he has finally fallen asleep. She leans against the guardrail, waiting. Somewhere on the bookshelves are the rest of her textbooks. Out the window is the moon. And the truth is she could be anywhere; she could be anywhere at all.

CONVERSATION

The women, new *friends,* are gathered in the home of Mary Chickarella, or Chick, as she's known—one of the faster set, formally introduced to Dorothy at the club ballroom-dancing finals. There, Chick and her husband, Georgie, had Lindyed to a second, while Dorothy and Charles took a third with a waltz. The two had golfed since then, once or twice, though Chick's handicap, she'd be the first to tell you, was in the single digits—Mary "Chick" Chickarella one of the more frequent names engraved on the trophies and silver bowls in the glass case outside the ladies' lounge, even the huge Regional Cup with its ornate handle and tiny, twenty-four-karat-gold woman arrested in midswing on the top.

"It's going to be a rap session," Chick had said when she called Dorothy. "You know, about what's going on."

"Vietnam?" Dorothy had asked.

"The war? Are you into that?"

"No," said Dorothy, who wasn't, truly, though Frank's long hair and ID bracelet kept it close.

"My friend Jean's coming from Philadelphia," Chick continued. "She's a Big Sister there. It's quite a scene. She says you won't believe what comes up. Scratch the surface, she says, and it bleeds."

• • •

Dorothy arrives with flowers. She couldn't think what else to bring and Charles's garden is in full June bloom, iris and delphiniums, the geraniums that reseed and grow wild in the mulched paths. These are the days he disappears within it, Lucy at his side like a small, turbulent shadow. The other children are gone: Frank at college, Claudia backing out of the drive too quickly on her way to flag-twirling practice, or student council, or one of the endless clubs she has recently joined, anticipating, she says, the brutalities of college admission. Only Lucy remains, her glasses smudged and sideways, her knees bruised and scabbed. According to Piaget, she's in an exuberant cycle—nine to ten—though to Dorothy she remains a puzzle: restless, skinny as a twig, given to writing notes of apology and despair, often in verse. At times, Dorothy has found them slipped beneath their bedroom door, as if an urgent message has just been delivered from the front desk or principal. The last one, a poem, had been scratched in ink on the corner of a notebook page, lined and blue, then torn out and folded many times over. It was something about the earth tilting on its axis—she couldn't remember what else, she told Charles later. Get her a Feelings Jar, Charles said, he still of the opinion that this had helped Frank and Claudia and their constant squabbling.

172

God, don't remind me, Dorothy said, knowing too well that a Feelings Jar spelled disaster.

Chick's house is, as Dorothy would have guessed, an interesting color, set off from the other houses of the development by its suggestion of purple and its festive summer wreath—pussy willows and a tiny, tarnished bell attached to a dangling ribbon. At her hip stands a cement animal, a narrow, long-snouted dog with a gaping mouth. Within its jaws someone has wedged an ashtray, now congested, and a plastic rose.

Chick opens the door in golf skirt and top, her hair newly cropped and bleached.

"Dorothy!" she says. "Entrez!"

Chick turns and disappears into the foyer's darkness; Dorothy follows, a bit off-balance. She had expected light and air, houseplants, but here is a hint of the Orient, and the smell of something new—she might well turn the corner and find the other women sprawled on silk pillows, the air thick with a druggy, opiate smoke. She has read about this kind of thing, watched the evening news. But no, the women gathered in Chick's living room look fine, friendly enough. They sit on folding chairs pulled into a circle, the indigenous furniture pushed to the walls, bright green and hung with prints of birds.

"Sissy," Chick yells toward the next room, where a black woman in a white uniform appears intent on polishing an already gleaming mahogany table. "She's the last of us!"

"Am I late?" Dorothy asks, turning back to Chick. "I couldn't find the—"

"You're fine," Chick says. "Perfect."

She claps her hands.

"Ladies," she says. "Here's the Dorothy I mentioned. Terrific dancer. Three children, I think. Three?"

Chick looks at Dorothy, who is suddenly aware of Charles's flowers in her hands.

"And a husband," Chick adds.

"Here," Dorothy says, offering the bouquet to Chick.

"Gorgeous," Chick says, sniffing. "Sissy," Chick yells, though Sissy has magically appeared, drinks on a tray and the polishing rag slung over her shoulder. Chick passes her Dorothy's bouquet, then turns back to the group, who remain fixed where they are, as if waiting for attention to animate them.

"Hi, Dorothy," they say, released in unison.

"Hello, everyone," Dorothy says back. "Hello, Laura," she adds, recognizing Laura Rasmussen, a younger woman from the club, a good golfer, who smiles and waves, mouthing another hello. Chick pulls an empty chair from the circle and gestures for Dorothy to sit; the rest of the women, now distracted by Sissy's return, accept drinks from the tray and pass a mother-of-pearl bowl of cocktail nuts. The drinks are gin gimlets. The nuts an assortment, shelled and salted.

"Hello?" Chick says, clapping again. "Knock-knock?" The women quiet and turn toward her.

"Should we review?" Chick says. "To my left is Jean, our Big Sister."

Jean nods as she's introduced. She looks nothing like the other women in the circle. Her thick, graying hair has been tied into two braids with a kind of rainbow yarn and parted so evenly down the middle she might have used a knife. She wears dungarees and a patterned blouse, the sleeves rolled past her elbows as if earlier she had been kneading bread.

She looks at all of them and smiles. "Hello," she says.

"Hello," they say.

"So," she says. "Okeydokey," she says. "What are we here for? Has it been explained?"

"Let's get the names down first," Chick says.

"Oh," she says. "Right."

"I have the ball," says Chick, reaching beneath her chair to bring up a tennis ball.

"Fun and games?" Laura S. says.

There are apparently two Lauras: Laura S. and Laura R. The women's names are now spelled out on sticky labels and stuck over their breasts. Everyone has had a drink and been apprised of the following, known in the movement, Big

Sister explains, as our pledge of allegiance: There are no rules; there is no bad idea in a rap session; everything goes; Big Sister is the boss.

"So," says Chick, looking at all of them and crossing her legs, muscular, she'd be quick to tell you, from preferring to walk her daily eighteen holes and carrying her own bag. "Since I have the ball, I'll go first," she says.

"Great!" a few of them say.

"I had an abortion," Chick continues, her tone relatively unchanged. "No, I had two abortions. Both before I was twenty. Both before I met Georgie."

Big Sister tilts over to rub Chick's back, though it doesn't appear to be in need of rubbing. Chick bristles a bit. If her eyes are filled with tears, she hides it well.

"Sara?" she says, tossing the ball to Sara.

"Me?" Sara says, catching it.

"Yup," Chick says.

"I go next?" Sara says, holding the ball.

"If I throw it to you, you go next."

Sara, who sits directly across from Chick in a skirt and top more customarily found in South America, turns to Big Sister. "I thought there were no rules in a rap session," she says.

"Speak your mind," Big Sister says, and her voice booms out and settles over all of them like a silky parachute.

"I hate rules," Sara says. "That's the first thing.

And I feel like—God, this is hard—I feel like we always have to live by this bullshit protocol, these rules—"

"We?" Big Sister interrupts.

"Yeah. Us," Sara says.

"Here? In this circle? Or do you mean women in general?" Big Sister asks.

"Is it a rule we have to state the obvious?" Sara asks.

In time it will be revealed that Sara is the one woman among them with a graduate degree, and that though she had once believed this would elevate her above the noisy din, the degree did nothing more than require her to waste a few years in Boston, prolonging the inevitable.

"The inevitable?" Big Sister asks.

Sara's look could kill.

"The inevitable," she repeats. Then, more brightly, "Dorothy?"

"I'm sorry?" Dorothy says. She's heard her name but she'd been thinking, trying to picture Sara in the snows of Boston, her jeans frayed around ragged sneakers, her coarse shirt tucked into a waist cinched with a bright, handmade macramé belt. Dorothy had met women like Sara before, certain older friends of Claudia's, teachers Claudia brought home, requiring role models, she had told Dorothy, of a more appropriate kind. *Simpatico*, Claudia had said. *Capisce?*

Dorothy had been imagining Sara in the Boston

snow. "Oh yeah," Sara says, tossing the ball to Dorothy, "and I had an abortion, too."

That Dorothy is here and not at her weekly bridge game, that she has made several telephone calls to reschedule this and that, to find a fourth, to arrange a babysitter, is a bit of a puzzle to her. True, she had been flattered when Chick called, Chick of the faster set, a woman who turned heads when she walked into the clubhouse, her golf shoes clicking the flagstone as if she were dogged by maracas. (Chick rarely went without them: either worn or dangerously slung over one shoulder, laces cinched, spikes down.) Yet Dorothy has little to no idea what is now expected of her, what she could possibly add to the conversation. This is what Jean, the Big Sister, had called it: We've come here today to have a conversation, she had said, to rap our experiences, to find the words to our collective history.

It had been a stirring introduction, only dampened by the fact that Big Sister read from prepared notes and paused on occasion to bite the end of one braid, her shoulders cattywampus, as if they'd been cast in a defective mold. Still, *conversation* somehow bloomed when she spoke it, unfurling the possibility of other words of a richer kind: words packed into sentences as ornate and complicated as those found in closed books, words that zigged and zagged, bumped and ruptured, words she could crawl out of, or maybe into—*conversation* a forest thick with evergreen through which, she could now see, lay a suggestion of a path. There light, tempered and soft, sparkled, beckoning her forward.

"Where are we going?" Big Sister had said in conclusion. "Whence did we come?" And to this Maggie Sykes had spontaneously applauded, though she stopped, immediately, shifting in her hard, straight chair, patting her name tag as if comforting a baby at her breast.

It's a good feeling, Dorothy thinks, to catch a ball, a camp feeling, though she had never been, a summer feeling, regardless, something of promise in it—she might win!—the ball new and firm. She thinks of the pleasing sound of a tennis can being opened, the release of that air, the sigh of it, though she wouldn't call it a sigh, exactly, harder than a sigh, stronger, a gasp, maybe, or a gulp, or even—

"Dorothy?" Big Sister says.

"What?"

"Your turn," Big Sister says.

"Oh, right," Dorothy says. "Right," she says.

They are all of them staring. She sits in a ring of unfamiliar women and they are all of them staring at her, waiting for her to say—what? She is unused to this, unused to being watched or, rather, seen. The ballroom dancing lessons, offered by Vivian Foxe—who once, apparently, lived in New York and studied with Martha Graham—would be an antidote to this, she had told Charles, an attempt to break out, to twirl and dip, to have *fun,* she had said to him, fun something they had once had in spades, or at least occasionally. Hadn't they? Besides, the children would get a kick out of their parents' dancing and—why not? Black tie! Club championship! She had shown Charles the mimeographed page with the specifics: limited space, couples only, come as you are (in formal attire), strap your dancing shoes on.

The night of the first lesson they had dressed in their fancy clothes: Charles in his military tuxedo, Dorothy in a sequined dress she had found years earlier at the Junior League Stop & Swap and bought on a whim. It had been a dark night, predictably, with the bluish March moon, too chilly to forget a wrap. Charles had linked his arm in hers and led her down the stone walk, breaking away only to open her door of the station wagon, to bend with a flourishy bow as if earlier the station wagon were a pumpkin and he a mouse. The children, or rather Lucy (Claudia had something else to practice, though she wished them well. Have a wonderful time! she had said, speeding off. Break a leg!), clapped and clapped, watching. She stood silhouetted with the babysitter in the light of the hallway chandelier, the front door open, the two flanked by the ghoulish shadows of twin rhododendrons. Dorothy looked up to see Lucy raise a shaky hand, the babysitter's arm linked and tight around her thin shoulder. Earlier, when Lucy had heard they were going, she had curled into a soft ball beneath the dining room table, refusing to move, refusing to budge, so that it did not surprise Dorothy to find her crumpled note crammed into the beaded clutch she carried. This before they got there, as she searched for a cigarette to calm her nerves. The note, written on a tear from a brown grocery bag, took some time to unfold.

"I am a hollow bone," it said, the *o*'s shaped into sad smiley faces, so that, in the dark of the automobile, Dorothy had to read it twice to be sure.

"Dorothy?" This now Big Sister.

"Yes?"

"Remember our pledge of allegiance?" she says.

"I am a hollow bone," Dorothy says.

Big Sister leans forward, craning around to look Dorothy eye to eye. "You are a hallowed bone?" she says, the room deadly silent, though Maggie Sykes, the unanimously elected recording secretary (there had been no challengers), scribbles notes.

"Hollow," Dorothy says. " 'Hollow bone.' "

"Oh," Big Sister says, pulling back. "A hollow bone."

"Did everyone hear that?" she says, looking around the circle, looking to Maggie Sykes. "Did everyone hear Dorothy's contribution?"

The group nods, although a few are distracted by a sudden grating mechanical sound—a backhoe? a dump truck?—out the opened bay windows.

"Sissy!" Chick yells, but Sissy is already there, cranking the levers closed, drawing the draperies across the light. She circles the furniture to click on individual lamps: a floor one with beaded glass, a large hooded bottle containing a ship, a small antique, its shade fluted into pleats. In the gradual dawning, the women turn back to Dorothy to hear what else, their eyes deep and unblinking, as if carved from wood or cast in bronze and gilded. They are panels on an ancient, intricate door, fifteen feet tall, top to bottom, with an iron knocker and brass nails. They guard a vault of impossible treasure or a Renaissance baptistery; no doubt they stand for something biblical, tell a riveting story, though perhaps one needs the headphones to understand.

The tennis ball rests in the cradle of Dorothy's lap, furry and uncomplicated and impossibly bright. Don't rush into silence, Big Sister had said. Our history, she had said, resides in silences.

Sara had snickered at this, but then again, Sara had snickered so often that Chick had asked if she were allergic and should Sissy put the dog out?

"Dorothy?" This now Chick, impatient.

"Yes?"

"Are you with us?"

"I'm here," Dorothy says.

"If you're finished, you might want to toss the ball," Chick says.

"Oh," says Dorothy. "I can toss it now?"

"There are no rules," says Chick. "But you might."

"Am I finished?"

"If you'd like to be," Chick says.

Dorothy picks up the ball. "Should I toss it?"

"I'm here," Chick says, holding out her hands to catch.

"You want it again?" Dorothy says.

"I could go again," Chick says, leaning forward, hands reaching. "There's no rule that I can't."

The first thing you would say about her husband, Georgie, is that he's a natural dancer, slim-waisted, broad-shouldered, a bit of a resemblance to Gene Kelly, if you were looking for that. Suffice it to say, he has a kind of feminine style. Always had. By that I mean, Chick adds, he's a dresser. Likes his spats, his trousers pressed.

"I've never seen the man in jeans," she says. "And also, he's easy to talk to."

The women cross their ankles, their flats kicked off and carried by Sissy back to the foyer, where they are paired and lined in rows: Pappagallos in various colors, sandals with daisies chiseled in the cowhide or bright artificial flowers attached to the straps. Now in the soft glow of the lighted room the women's feet, bare and colored at the toes, caress the Corsican rug. They have had another round of drinks; they are trying to think of what to say next.

"We married the day after graduation. You know, everybody did that sort of thing then. Boom boom. Georgie had a certain light in his eyes. I won't say I didn't fall head over heels. I did, God help me. Head over heels. So he popped the question and we got married. The day after graduation, I already told you. Boom boom. The day after that, I mean *the day after that,* he told me he prefers boys. Just so. Boom boom. Matter-of-fact and how-do-you-do. Mary, he said—I was Mary then, a good Catholic girl, you know—he said, Mary, I must tell you. I prefer boys. Which is not to say he couldn't, just that he preferred the other. I mean, he wanted to make his preferences known."

Here Chick pauses as if to take a sip of water, but there is no water, only a pitcher of gin, and they've finished that, and so she holds out her empty glass. "Sissy," she yells, and Sissy is there, her bright white uniform stark as she leans to refill Chick's glass from a bottle.

"Jesus, would you give her a break?" Sara says.

"What?" Big Sister says.

"I'm talking to Miss Diarrhea of the Mouth. I'm saying, 'Tell Sissy to sit, already.' Let's invite her in. Let's see what Sissy has to say."

The women in the circle turn from Chick to Sissy to Big Sister to Sara, who reaches over and plucks the ball from Chick's lap, tossing it too quickly in Sissy's direction. It spins then plonks the empty pitcher on the drinks tray.

"Game point," says Laura S., lighting a cigarette.

"I could take a load off," Sissy says.

"Take a load off," Sara says, standing up and offering her chair.

"Sit here, Sissy."

"I'm Sister," Sissy says.

"Sister," says Sara, pointing to Sissy, "and Big Sister," says Sara, pointing to Jean.

"Never were there such delightful sisters," sings Laura S. She smiles and blows some smoke out.

"We're getting off subject," Big Sister says.

"What's happening?" Chick says. "I'm not finished."

"Go on," says Big Sister. "It's all good."

"I was telling you about Georgie," Chick says.

"We're listening. We're still listening," Big Sister says. Someone asks for the nuts, and the mother-of-pearl bowl is passed counterclockwise toward the requester.

Chick begins again, and then she does not; she'll desist, she says. She'll peter out. "Kaputt, Ich bin," she says. "Ich bin kaputt."

"You were talking about Georgie's preferences," Big Sister says, encouraging.

"As per boys," Sara says, "as in, not you."

"I've lost my place is the point," Chick says.

"Ditto," Beverly says, somewhere in the dark.

"You're here?" Chick says, squinting. "Bev?"

"Present," Bev says.

"My darling," Chick says, scooting forward on her folding chair, inching toward the tennis ball with her big toe to push it weakly in Beverly's direction. "Join us," she says.

The afternoon waxes and wanes—the ball lost, eventually, hidden in one of Chick's sneakers by Sara on her way to the powder room.

Now it's Faith's turn, her voice issuing up from the living room, rising and falling as she describes her delivery—how she was strapped to the bed and cinched tight with buckled leather belts; how she was held down as if she were insane. No one ever said that they would do that. "I mean, no one ever said," she said. "Did anyone ever say that?"

"They don't tell you," Laura R. adds. "They don't tell you any—"

"Ruptions," Big Sister says, "come from inter-rupt—"

"They gave me a shot of something," Faith continues, "then they all left the room. Like they had a train to catch, or a curtain. They shut the little door, and no one was there at all. I couldn't move. They left the lights on, all the lights, and the shot made me sweat and shake, and the baby—it smelled like garlic. Not the baby but the whole room. Someone must have had it for dinner. And when the doctor came in, he was talking about a television program, and he didn't even look at me, say hello—"

"God, when Michael was born, I swore like a trucker. I mean, the language!" Chick has slipped off her chair and sprawls on the Corsican rug, an ashtray at her elbow. "And of course Georgie was off somewhere, with some orderly, no doubt."

"Chick," Big Sister says.

"Or maybe a male nurse."

"Chick," Big Sister says.

"I'll shut it," Chick says.

"Button it," Big Sister says.

"I'll button it," Chick says.

Sissy snorts a laugh. "Like hell," she says. She sits cross-legged on the folding chair, the mother-of-pearl bowl in her lap, the white uniform stretched above her knees. She's untied her shoes and slipped them off her feet. She has had a drink, and she might have another. "Being off duty," she had said in Chick's direction. "Being invited to participate," she had said. Sara sits on the floor in front of Sissy, leaning back against the legs of Sissy's chair, toe to toe with Chick. Earlier, they played footsie—Ph.D. against Married-to-a-Homosexual, Sara had proposed, though, she said, it was an unfair match, really, Chick already up two abortions to one. This before the break, when Big Sister had asked for a moment of silence and then invited them all to stand—shoulder to shoulder, as it were, bone to bone.

"Let's hear how far we've come," Big Sister had said. "To hear your words in the voice of another is extraordinarily empowering," she said. "Let's celebrate our commonalities," she said. Then she invited Maggie Sykes to step forward to recite—in random order, please—the minutes, Maggie Sykes making what appeared to be a unilateral decision to push through the circle and stand smack on the bull's-eye. She raised her notepad to an easier reading distance and, with shaky hands, cleared her throat.

"Beverly P.," she boomed, "having to do with invisibility, childhood in fortress of tied sticks—symbolic?—circumstances of mother's hospitalization; Chick—abortions, Georgie's homosexuality, self-esteem? undermining, like a trick knee; Laura S.—the questions asked in the workplace, advances (re: sexual) by older brother (Harrison) inappropriate vis-à-vis boys will be boys, or, possibly, criminal?; Laura R.—laundry, et cetera; Maggie—definition of frigid? what is considered normal?; Laura S.—we are our own enemies, listen to us!; Sara—graduate degree bullshit? academy bullshit? abortion, entire discussion bullshit? our privilege to ask, our privilege of speech, our privilege of voice re: Sister; Sister—industrial-military (son in Indochina) complex; Dorothy—hollow bone."

The words "hollow bone" were the last read before Maggie Sykes lowered her notes, the *o*'s dissipating like smoke rings, wafting over the group as they were instructed to sit down and resume their former positions.

"I thought I was dead," Faith continues. "I thought I had come to die. I did die. I was out of myself. I was in a corner shouting and no one could hear me, and then I screamed and screamed and screamed and no one could hear me, and it was only after they took me off the stuff, I mean took the needles out, Annie in the nursery, that I saw they all had plugs in their ears. Every one of them. Plugged ears."

How the day ended is a bit of a fog, though Dorothy knows that she lined up with the rest to thank Big Sister and to shake her hand, and that she had inexplicably hugged Laura Rasmussen, feeling a sudden kinship and promising to invite Laura and her husband to dinner. Sister she tipped five dollars. "Unnecessary," Sister said, though she folded the bill and tucked it into the shoulder of her uniform.

Dorothy walked out into the last of the June day, the brightness disarming, assaulting, even, as if all of them had been huddled in a cave. Chick bent just beyond, deadheading a pot of daisies, flicking the dried blossoms into the yard like so many spent cigarettes. Beside her the dog gnawed the tennis ball.

Perhaps Chick had already forgotten her guests, or maybe they had just disappointed her. Hard to tell, really—she was pretty, Chick, and a terrific golfer: practically a scratch handicap, regional champion three years running. She would win several more tournaments before leaving the area, asked to resign from the club, its rules firm on the question of divorcées. Still her name remained for years on the trophies outside the ladies' lounge before one by one her titles were defeated.

Why Dorothy thinks of all of this now, she has no idea: it seems inappropriate to daydream here, Charles in his box before her, Lucy and Claudia and even Frank returned with their own families, sitting like so many cowed supplicants on either side of the pew. But then, everyone has been remembering something: business colleagues, golfing buddies, a cousin, more like a brother, limping up to tell childhood stories; now their old pastor drones on, reciting predictable passages. She will be the last to go, it's been decided, though for the spouse to speak is entirely against protocol, they have said; it would be fine, they said, if she never uttered a word.

She is happy to break protocol, she tells them. Entirely delighted. Break, break, break, she says. Smash smash smash. Besides, she says, who but she could recount that Charles was a terrific dancer?

"Now here's a talent!" barked Vivian Foxe. "Absolutely terrific!" she shouted, as Dorothy and Charles waltzed in the way she had taught them.

But first, the couples—a few who looked familiar, and Chick and Georgie, whom everyone sort of knew—were led into the club ballroom and told to form a circle. Vivian Foxe held up a finger for silence, then clicked over to the stage and unsheathed a record album, fitting it onto the turntable. She lifted the arm as the record revolved, timing the needle to the groove. In an instant, scratches etched the quiet—then, remarkably, the music. The music! she might tell them. Sounds without words! There were chords and phrases, refrains, rifts, and solos building, then not, then dismantled and built, again, and again, the all of it filling the voluminous ballroom, sweeping them up as a tide would, spilling them onto a different shore: Charles in his military tuxedo, she in sequins and gloves.

"Let's begin!" Vivian Foxe shouted, clapping her hands. "Ladies' choice!"

And as she reached for Charles's hand, the note she still held—she had forgotten!—slipped like a secret message to the polished ballroom floor. "I am a hollow bone" is what it read, though now, remembering it, Dorothy wonders what Lucy had meant to tell her, wonders what any of them were trying to say.

SHE WAS
LIKE THAT

Sharon Peterson angles to the empty space in front of the hydrant and brakes, hazards engaged, wipers at high speed.

"Hey," she calls across the cluttered front seat, window cracked though the rain rakes in—the storm too sudden, too much: one of those late spring tempests out of nowhere.

"What?" This Ginny: drippy, frazzled: Sharon a stranger. "I'm sorry, what?"

Sharon releases the lock and pushes the now-wet papers to the seat well, papers she'll let dry and grade later or maybe, next week, or maybe, not at all. "Avanti!" she says. She pulls up the handle and pushes open the door.

"God, thank you. Wow. That's really nice," Ginny says, getting in. She shakes closed her three-dollar umbrella, no match for this weather. "Wow," she says, turning to Sharon. "You are *so* nice," she says. "Really," she says, as if someone has disagreed, slamming the car door shut like at any moment Sharon Peterson will change her mind.

But Sharon Peterson won't change her mind. She feels her heart soar, its wings muddied, true, and yet somehow closer to the sun or rather a certain warmth. This is the best thing I have ever done, Sharon Peterson thinks as she puts the car in drive, as Ginny buckles up.

Serendipity, spontaneity, recklessness: Sharon Peterson's mother would have called it a break for freedom. She had once done the same, boarding a Greyhound for Penn Station close to 5:00 a.m., ending up near the lions on the steps of the main branch of the New York Public Library, not such a long walk from Port Authority she said once home, near midnight, and besides the day was grand. She ate a tuna fish sandwich on whole wheat she had packed for the road and a paper bag of peanuts purchased from the vendor at the first crosswalk, a man, she liked to recall, who pushed back the pocket change she held out to him. "Too beautiful a day for money," he said.

Divine, the City, she said: All those different-color people. And the tulips!

So, there's her mother by way of example, and Woolf, of course: always Woolf. The Virginia of the constant wanderings: trench coat buckled or rather sashed, her breaks for freedom less exotic or far-ranging, her breaks for freedom meandering the gloomy streets of London in search of, what? A pencil? Sharon pictures her this way, Woolf's face the face from that famous photograph: hair in a chignon, nose sharp, eyes wise even in profile or at least, cast down, away from the photographer, the view: dun-colored windows; or, rotting fruit in the apple orchard, a graffitied brick wall; maybe, the bloody butcher passing or the fat cook; maybe, the insolent child with the pony wondering what all the fuss is about, why this woman in her long skirts as if: important.

Sharon knows the essay cold, could recite it at length, trotting out Woolf, her Woolf, like a brilliant, dotty auntie summoned from her garret study down the creaking stairs. First the swoosh of that long skirt, the soft button-up boots on the stairwell treads, and then the tremendous presence: Sharon asking Woolf to recite whatever she might deem necessary for spiritual backup in the classroom, as others in her department summon the Gospels or Zora Neale Hurston: Woolf her in-house intellectual; her proof that a meandering mind might better explicate the mysteries of life than a mind that seeks to reach its point.

"What if your Woolf is not my Woolf," the impertinent one, Tina, had asked just yesterday, the spring light slanting into the Milbank classroom in the way the spring light has slanted into the Milbank classroom for years, Sharon preferring this seminar room above the others for the light and the one round wooden table, heavy-legged, oak, scratched with the meanderings of a thousand Woolf descendants.

Several of them pierce themselves with small,

metal rods through their ears and eyebrows and tongues—Tina of this lot. She lisped when she spoke, her eyes a challenge. On the midsemester evaluations Tina wrote: Professor Peterson is neither exciting nor horrifying. She is as bland as a sock. Although it was anonymous, Sharon recognized the tone.

Another passenger, Miranda, now sits in back, a baby strapped to her chest, a Fairway bag on her lap like a toddler. She was caught off guard, she had explained to Sharon and Ginny, her phone dead, the subways flooded and God knows.

Yes, Ginny said. That's it exactly.

And then they brake again. The guy has stepped from the curb and is swaying like the last duckpin. He appears to want to flag an occupied cab—is he a tourist? Difficult to tell. The rain falls in watery sheets as if staged rain in a theatrical production. People run like all get-out, catapulting over puddles, huddling into clots in doorways as delivery guys wearing garbage bags pedal past on shaky bicycles.

"Where's the fire?" Sharon Peterson calls.

"What?" the guy says, closer.

"Quick," Ginny says.

"Really?" the guy says. He's getting them all wet.

"Hurry up," Miranda says from the back seat.

"Great," the guy says. "Okay," he says.

Miranda resettles the Fairway bag as the guy scoots across, introducing himself as Fred Vegas, as in the town; Miranda, Miranda says, as in the tragedy.

"This is my daughter, Little Miranda," she says. "Sometimes I call her el Diablo."

"I've got three," Fred Vegas says.

"Three's the new two," Miranda says.

"Music?" Sharon asks. "Or would everyone prefer news?"

She loves the "everyone" and could idle all day. She adjusts the side view and waits for the traffic to let up before pulling back onto Amsterdam—difficult to see what's what in this foggy glass and a full car to consider. Passengers! The traffic's horrendous but Amsterdam looks clear, she tells them. Nothing like Amsterdam, she says. She was on Madison earlier and, really? Madison? What's with Madison? she says. It's all about the West Side. Take the intersection of Peter Jennings Way and Columbus, or Humphrey Bogart Place and West End; Edgar Allan Poe Street and Broadway. All the artists and the Canadians are on the West Side, she tells them. Who's over there? Dag Hammarskjöld?

"Duke Ellington," Fred Vegas says. "My parents were swing dancers. Duke Ellington Boulevard, around 106th and Broadway. West End."

"Exactly," Sharon says, slowing to comply

199

with the light, the radio on the station Fred Vegas has suggested, no one voting news, *please never again news,* the music jazzy, a breeze—saxophone or clarinet or French horn. Sharon eyes the corralled automobiles behind her: a temporary, nervous peace, all of them eager to accelerate again, to get there. And then she checks her back seat passengers. Fred Vegas has turned his attention to Miranda to converse in parent—the business of discipline, getting in/getting out, sleepaway camps, lice checks.

Somebody honks. "Highty-ho," Sharon says, finding she is blocked. A stalled car in front of her overrun by crisscrossing pedestrians: at any moment one might leap on the hood and do an Irish jig or hit the fender and somersault through the air. Just last block a man in a winter coat stood in the middle of the bike lane, arms outstretched, head back, as if a chicken in the rain. "It's called driving," she yells, swerving to pass the stalled car. "It's called using your brain," she yells.

Her passengers go quiet. All right. A few blocks of thought is entirely called for; this can happen in the rain and often does. Call it contemplation. But at Eighty-ninth she can't stand the silence. "Fred Vegas?" she calls back. "Knock knock?"

"Present!" Fred Vegas says.

"Where would you like to be delivered?"

"Who cares?" he says, as Miranda leans in. "I read in San Francisco," she says, "drivers put some sort of crazy thing on their hood—a furry mustache, something—that means they wouldn't be averse to you flagging them down. It costs something but still. Very California. Funny."

"I'll accept no currency," Sharon says as Miranda leans back, although not before she offers mints.

"Would the front seat occupants enjoy a mint?" Miranda says.

Sharon stretches out her arm, opening her palm in the way of her father on cross-country trips—she had forgotten: her father insisting as she hoarded her small bag of potato chips or strings of black licorice, his favorite.

"Where did you get that?" Miranda asks.

Sharon keeps her eyes on the double-parked Poland Spring truck—coals to Newcastle but still the men diligently unload, quickly unload. "What?" she says, although she knows exactly: the tattoo, a Chinese character on her pulse point or what Carl had called her inseam, faded now but still there, a weak blue.

"It means forgiveness," she says, although it doesn't, actually. It never did.

Three boys on her side and three girls on his; people commented. She and Carl became a popular couple, the Brady Bunch. But the children grew and scattered as children will, someone always relocating to Asia or London,

Hong Kong (banking); holidays a work of art: exes elsewhere. She started her Christmas lists in July. Of course, she should add, no, or rather, not exactly. Things are always not exactly. First, too many fights. Drugs. Once they opened the front door to see the doorman holding Casey, passed out cold, in his arms. He lifted her up to them as if in offering and even at the time Sharon had thought of the Pietà, had thought there was something oddly angelic about Carl's middle child, a slip of a girl, white as carved alabaster against the doorman's dark suit, a thin strand of brown hair caught in her mouth. She had retched for hours in the powder room. Neither of them said a word.

But here she was going *on,* she said to the stranger. What must he think of her? Sharon looked around the middle-of-the-day bar; one of those invisible places on every block, the kind never seen until accidentally found. This one of the many forgettable places after Carl's death— how had she made her way to York?

She reached for her drink, watery. "Look at that," he said and she knew but did not turn to look. Wouldn't expect that, the stranger did not continue. He had his own problems. Must be a story in that, the stranger did not say.

She let him be, pretending to watch the television hanging above the bar, the one on the far end; the near-end television too close. On the television something was happening somewhere that required everyone's immediate attention. The whirl of it nauseated her. She should have had breakfast or dinner, even, but she had reached the age of cheese and crackers, occasionally a bowl of Grape-Nuts: all those years, all those children, all those students and papers to grade. Casey in the doorman's arms, that sweet face, the strand of brown hair. Chicken parts washed and grilled, washed and broiled. She would rather eat a good book. Thomas Hardy for dinner, Willa Cather for dessert. Mrs. Dalloway her Thanksgiving meal: her Virginia; her wanderer.

" 'What kind of deal can you give a senior?' I asked when I walked in."

"You didn't!" Fred Vegas says. Sharon has pulled to the far corner of Ninety-sixth and Amsterdam, the bus stop, to finish the story— they asked for details! She had found the tattoo parlor in Brooklyn, a grimy storefront wedged between a Chinese restaurant and a neon pizza parlor. Old news, the affair, but she had somehow forgotten to mention it to Carl.

Sometimes you just need a dramatic gesture, she says. Sometimes you need to *do something*. She believed Carl would appreciate the permanence, and anyway, anyway, didn't she have to confess before he forgot who she was and forgot who he was? It was an experiment in education, she told him; the unexamined life and so forth. Nothing more. A visiting fellow, one of those wry Swedish types—Woolf chose women, she chose a man, but either way, it had to do with exploration, no? Meandering? A Break for Freedom?

Think of all the things you miss when you know too clearly where you're going, I told him.

She does not add how Carl sat in his favorite chair in the maid's room off the hallway, the one they had converted to a den, near the globe on the stand that, before all this, all that, they would nightly consult for dinner—spinning the globe blind, any body of water default Japanese. It's such a tiny island, Carl would say. We have to increase its odds. All other countries fair game: They'd traveled to the outer boroughs for Tibetan and Bengalese; Queens for Greek, Indian. Once they drove clear across the GW Bridge in search of Chilean.

There is a heavy, humid silence in the car among her passengers, as if at any moment a white orchid might bloom from the dashboard, or a raincloud burst overhead.

"Well," Fred Vegas finally says, "I like," he says. "Very au courant," he says.

He reaches forward to shake Sharon's hand, his smile wide. "It's been a pleasure, Professor Peterson. Thank you for the ride."

"Me, too," Miranda says. "Thank you," she

says, scooting out after Fred Vegas, the baby and the Fairway bag like twin barnacles, clinging as she slams the door hard with her free hand and disappears into the soggy crowd. And now the back seat feels like an empty room off a hallway lined with cardboard boxes, one marked sweaters, another, knickknacks. Goodwill called to schedule the pickup from that same doorman in the lobby, always their favorite after the Casey debacle, still guarding, still vigilant for what might come next.

"Professor Peterson?" Ginny says.

"I'm sorry," Sharon says. "Drifting," she says. "A liability of age," she says. The sound the metronome blink of the hazards and farther still an ambulance, the rain returned, the reprieve into which Fred Vegas and Miranda just escaped that: a reprieve.

She had almost forgotten her other passenger.

"What happened next?" the woman asks as Sharon tries to recall her name—Jane? Tina? Something predictable: as bland as a sock.

"Right," Sharon says. "Skulls up and down her arms, the young girl at the counter. I couldn't take my eyes off. Some wrapped in snakes and then on her chest a skeleton with saddlebags and spurs. She shows me this greasy book, like a diner menu. Chinese characters. Hundreds."

"Not like the Phoenicians," the woman interrupts. "I always think about that: twenty-six characters. Shakespeare and everything."

"Anyway," Sharon continues. "This girl says she'll ask in back. She doesn't know any meanings, she says. Isn't that funny?—but she'll ask in back and so she goes in back and then returns and says her boss thinks this one's *adoration* and this one, and she points, he's pretty sure is *wisdom*."

"So wisdom but no forgiveness."

Sharon stares out the rainy window to where the wipers, briefly, sporadically, in rhythm, swish clear a view before the water again blinds.

"Nope," she says. "No forgiveness."

Religion has never really been her thing, Sharon tells Patience Remington, picked up after Ginny—that was it—took advantage of another pause to unfurl her broken umbrella and sprint across the street, leaving Sharon to idle near the Cathedral of Jesus Christ, a pretty stone church on the next corner, red geraniums in window boxes and a red-painted door. She had been considering continuing to Duke Ellington Boulevard given the jazzy radio station and in honor of Fred Vegas's parents when she spied Patience Remington, a large woman in a bright yellow suit, hurrying down the church steps to flag the M11, which clearly had no intention of noticing.

"Church on Sundays with a father who sang in the choir, and a mother who refused everything on principle and took Sunday mornings to fish," Sharon says. "Catch and release, of course. Mom wasn't a hunter."

"Is that right?" Patience Remington says. She sits in the front seat, the wet newspaper she used as an umbrella folded in her wide lap.

She'd love a ride north to 153rd or thereabouts, she had said to Sharon's offer. Just close enough to skip the bus. No hurry at all, she had said to Sharon's suggestion that they might first pass by Duke Ellington Boulevard given the general direction.

"That's fine," Patience Remington had said.

"This is Ohio. Have you been to Ohio?" Sharon asks, Patience Remington offering up she had relatives in Sandusky, which had always felt to her like a better name for a soda than a town. Bee-bop, Sandusky Pop!

"Agreed!" Sharon says, brightening. Duke Ellington Boulevard a disappointment, just another city pocket, an intersection of gray brick and filthy limestone apartment buildings bordering an adjacent small park. Straus Park, Sharon happens to know, named after the famous Strauses who went down on the *Titanic*. Also, she says, every anniversary of the sinking of the *Titanic* a small band of New Yorkers march around the park with homemade instruments. She saw it once: grown-ups like preschoolers, shaking rice in oatmeal cans and whacking drum sticks on garbage lids. "With my own eyes," she says.

"Is that right," Patience Remington says.

"Apparently they were very well known at the time," Sharon says.

"The Strauses," she adds.

Patience Remington refolds the newspaper.

"So, religion," Sharon says, turning back onto Broadway. She'll take the highway to save time, left on 125th—"the odds go to New Jersey"— and merge from there onto the Henry Hudson.

"We'd join Mom after services," she continues. "She would row back to the shore and pick us up and we would get in and she would row us out to the middle of the lake, me in my Sunday dress, Dad in his suit. Mom wore suspenders. She was like that. She had these braids she twisted on the top of her head; you rarely see that style anymore. A Scotsman or two in the bloodline—she'd dive for a penny if she ever saw one on the street and she had to have her tea on the boil. Always. Fishing, I don't know. I guess it was something to do."

"Amen to that," says Patience Remington. She looks out toward the granite ledge that lines the highway.

"Plus, on my first communion," Sharon says, "Stephanie Blake got a star sapphire necklace and I got nothing."

"Oh, Lord," Patience Remington says.

Later still, after the rain stops for good and the sun sets, again, Sharon Peterson lands outside the city limits in one of those towns along the river whose names sound vaguely historical or poetic, as if only yesterday horses trotted along their dirt paths or were tied, in pairs, to the split-rail fence of the post office: Sleepy Hollow, Dobbs Ferry.

Harry, she believes the man said by way of introduction, or, possibly, Henry, his eyes tiny pinpricks of light, tunneling to the smallest denominator, refusing to budge. His line of work involves air compressors, he told her. She does not know a thing about that, she says.

He says, no, she wouldn't.

She says, her line of work is specific to Virginia Woolf and does he know Woolf?

He's heard of her, he said.

She teaches college girls, she says. Then, college women, she says.

I have daughters, he says.

Words and more words—she does not say. Layers, depth, she does not say. Confluence, she does not say, although at other times she has found herself quoting one of her own well-honed lectures, wondering if what she had to say about any of it might still be of interest. She swishes her watery drink and thinks of Woolf. Day after day, week and then month, the drink and the rain eddying around her as if she were a boulder in a river, or a pebble in a sink. And she had only been in search of a pencil.

Or forgiveness.

Or perhaps a tug of something: something tangible from the deep, something like a hello from somewhere, from one of the other creatures of the sea.

SLOW THE HEART

Maggie suggests they play the game the Obamas used to play in the White House at dinner. (She read it!) Roses and Thorns, she explains to Peter and Grace; the good things of the day the roses and the bad things of the day the thorns.

They're in the kitchen, at the white Formica table, the light overhead flickering and too blue—"But let's cut the thorns," Maggie says to the two of them, no longer little-little though still children, certainly, still capable of games. "I mean seriously, why thorns? Aren't there enough thorns now in everyday everything? I say we change the rules for our dinner table."

"Jesus, Mom," Grace says. She's been arranging her lo mein into lopsided circles on her plate. "Lighten up."

"Exactly," Maggie says. She looks from Grace back to Peter back to Grace. "See, this is my point. Let's lighten up. No more news. No more thorns: at this table, we will be genetically modified. Thorn-less: A genetically modified, thorn-less family."

"Crikey!" says Peter, who since Will left has claimed to be an Australian orphan named Captain Flick.

"I'll start," Maggie says. "Peter's smile is my

rose. He is my rose tonight. Tonight there is nothing better than Peter's smile."

"I'm Flick," Peter says.

"That's dopey. Peter can't be your rose," Grace says, pushing the noodles to the edge of her plate. "A rose isn't a smile. You said it's a thing. It's supposed to be a thing. A smile isn't a thing."

"Yes, it is," Maggie says. "A smile can be a thing."

"A stupid thing," Grace mutters. She stares out the kitchen window at the westward expanse: water tanks and ladders climbing water tanks, glassy high-rises, roiling sunset clouds, cirrus, Maggie thinks, so not exactly roiling, more fragile than roiling, composed entirely, she happens to know, of ice, cirrus clouds breaking across our Mary Poppins view, as Will used to say, or, rather, sing, when the children were little-little—*Chim chiminey, chim chiminey, chim chim cher-ee.* Grace slowly exhales, expanding her tiny rib cage with no doubt intention and peace, directing her breath to slow the heart. This is how Grace explained it in Group. Important to slow the heart, she said. The Buddhist monks do, she said. Mrs. Palowski says at Harvard Medical School they have a whole course in the slowness of Buddhist monks' hearts. (Mrs. Palowski! Always Mrs. Palowski!) Also, at Harvard Medical School, they found marijuana cream cures cancer.

The monks? Maggie had said from her place

just beyond the circle, although no one had laughed, not even Will, who sat across from her.

Now Grace looks back at Maggie and sets her eyes in that expression she sometimes gets, the dead-end look. "I'm not playing" is what she says.

Maggie might scream. She might beat her fists against the kitchen table and scream. Not *playing?* Remember, *Yahtzee?* Remember, *Clue?* Remember, *Monotony?* You *always* play, Maggie might scream. Play!

But she doesn't scream. Instead, she smiles the mother smile that fools no one, looking out toward the Mary Poppins view and thinking gratitude and peace, exhaling her own breath, willing her own heart to slow. "It will be fun," she says.

The Obamas thought it was fun—(she read it)—and it *could* be—she and Grace and Peter playing Roses and Thorns, the children regaling one another with fun stories from school, adventures in plaid and gray, thick maroon sweaters rolled past those beautiful, blue-veined wrists. Fun stories told here in their apartment kitchen with its stuttering light, the array of Chinese takeout on the white Formica table she and Will, then fun newlyweds, lugged up from the sidewalk, cluttered with open take-out containers and small plastic cups of mysterious, glutinous sauces.

They have ordered in again, Maggie late at work. Back by 7:00, she had texted. Requests? Peter wanting his favorite: garlic string beans he feeds to the cat. Grace agreeing to lo mein, though of course she has eaten none. Maggie watched as she pushed most of her portion into the paper napkin in her lap.

"No can do," Grace says, Peter looking from his sister to his mother to his sister as if trying to spin a web, something sticky and long lasting that will permanently bind them, something with a sprinkle of fairy dust and rainbows to forever guide their tricky crossings.

Will did not seem particularly bothered by Captain Flick. This yesterday, when he dropped off the children from the weekend and said, uncharacteristically, yes to her offer of tea. They sat in the kitchen, the day darker, clouds a mottled, heavy white. Maggie asked Will if he were bothered by their son's new accent, the fictitious autobiography, the ridiculous Australian name. Had he noticed all this strangeness? she said as she poured out the tea. Had he even noticed?

"Of course I noticed," Will said.

Captain Flick was orphaned at a young age and grew up with goats on a hillside somewhere outside of Sydney, like Heidi, Peter had explained. ("No goats in Australia," Grace said.

"Only sheep.") The goats, however, were nothing compared to the tragic deaths of Captain Flick's parents. All very Roald Dahl: a snorkeling mishap, a white shark, blood in the water, bits of flesh, and a torn life preserver. ("You let him watch too much YouTube," Grace said.)

Will sipped his tea and listened, his eyes shadowy as if he hadn't had the sleep he needed or maybe he had been having a lot of sex. Have you been having a lot of sex? Maggie wanted to ask, but she stuck to Captain Flick as Will listened, sifting a packet of Sweet'n Low into his tea.

"You remember my mother's famous story" is what he said, stirring. And she did, of course. She remembered his mother's famous story, how his mother sat in the corner at school and blinked all day, the entire day, blink, blink, blink, refusing to budge, refusing to do anything but blink. She remembered that, she could tell him. She remembered that as she remembered a lot of things, although sex, if they're on the subject, now only dimly. She's on leave, she told Cate in Portland, who said a woman in her department bought an orgasm every morning before work. It's a chain, Cate said. Like Staples. It opens at 6:00 a.m. Entirely anonymous. You just walk in, she said, Maggie listening and trying to picture it, although all she could picture was her gynecologist's examining room, his collection of

Maine landscapes on the walls, the sound of his metal stool as he rolled up to the steel table where she waited, her discarded *Vogue* somewhere beside her, knees up, paper gown already ripped at the plastic tie.

So, yes, she remembered Will's mother's famous story like she remembered a lot of things: how, for instance, Will now lived with his college roommate's sister in Baltimore, where his college roommate's sister ran a yoga practice and Will had moved his law practice, the two of them practicing their practices all day. She remembered also how she would love to scratch his eyes out but, then again, she remembered that she still loved him, or so she told the children, who had wanted to know if she still loved him in that nice, old wife kind of we're-still-family way.

And yes, and yes, there are still good guys—great guys. Wonderful guys! She sees them on the city streets in the morning waiting with their children for the school bus or walking their dogs, golden retrievers and Labradors in pleasing autumnal colors. Good guys in Central Park tossing footballs and softballs and Frisbees and in restaurants on West Fourth holding wine lists in their good-guy hands. Some have shaved heads; others have gone bald; a few have full heads of hair, lion manes. Life suddenly, in this recalling, a Dr. Seuss story with good guys in all shapes and sizes and colors, great guys existing in spades across the city, across the globe, the globe practically teaming with great guys—like Obama, take Obama!—that wonderful great guy who made it his business, even as the president of the United States, not only to have dinner with his wife and children every evening at six o'clock but to play a game called Roses and Thorns— and were they still living under the same roof, were Will still the great guy she remembers, kind and attentive and curious, she would ask him about that thorn part, if he got what she meant about cutting out that thorn part, especially now, especially *now*. But Will is not the great guy she remembers. Will is a shit, she does not tell the children. A sonofabitch, she does not say.

"Just ignore," Will said.

"What?" Maggie said.

"Captain Flick. You asked me what I thought. Ignore it," he said. "That's what I do. He's more resilient than you think."

"All right," she said. She sat across from him. "Okay," she said.

Will held the lumpy cup their friend Jennifer had spun on her wheel and given them as a wedding present, a set of six, and sipped his tea.

"You think too much," he said.

There were originally six, in six colors, but someone broke the red along the way and then the brown although the brown was on purpose, Will one night—it was funny, actually—knocking

219

the brown one from the narrow arm of the living room chair. Poor little cup, he said, laughing; poor little ugly cup.

"I guess I do," she says.

"He's a Cancer," he says. "A crab. He's just building his shell. Maybe this is his fantasy life."

"Australia?" she says, and Will laughs—she knew he would—and then he puts down the bumpy cup on the white Formica table the two of them lugged up from the sidewalk all those fun years ago and tells Maggie what else: that he and yoga Caroline have decided to make it official, the date in June or maybe July so the children can spend the week. They are thinking at a resort in Colorado known for horses and mountains and really quite spectacular. Maggie listens to Will's description of the spectacular resort and then she does not: then she's remembering that time in college Will jumped the chain-link fence of those famous, manicured gardens near her parents' home, running in the twilight to the maze, an elaborate puzzle of shorn arborvitae monumental as Stonehenge.

It was cold, this near the holidays, everyone else wandering the grounds to see the festive trees, spruce and magnolia and beech lined with white and red and blue and yellow sparkling lights, the paths near the gargantuan glass conservatory jammed with dressed-up visitors and old people negotiating electric carts, knees blanket-covered.

"And Grace?" Maggie says when Will finally quits talking. "Should we ignore her too?"

"Let's start over," Maggie says.

"If I hadn't made the express at Fourteenth, I wouldn't have gotten to Forty-second when I did to switch to the local, and if I hadn't switched to the local, I wouldn't have run into Mimi Rocker—I know, her name." (Peter's giggles!) "Neither of you will remember but Mimi Rocker babysat a thousand years ago. She was someone's nanny's friend and she arrived with a parrot on her shoulder—"

"I remember," Grace says.

Maggie has turned off the flickering light for Peter's headache—"MSG," Grace said—the only light now in the kitchen from the hallway, a pool just beyond them; the day fast disappearing. Peter slips overboard into Maggie's lap, too tired for his chair, he says, his head flopped against her shoulder as he used to do as a toddler after the park playground, feet filthy from sand. She can feel his heat as she strokes his hair, rests her chin on his big hard skull. He is too big for her lap.

"Really?" Maggie says. "Yeah?"

"I remember the parrot," Grace says.

"You brilliant girl."

"I don't remember!" Peter says, twisting to accuse her.

"It was gross," Grace says. "It was covered in fleas. It bit them and chewed them all night long."

"I don't remember a parrot!" Peter says.

"You were just months old, Peter. Fleas? Really?"

"Flick, matey!"

"And she had them, too. She scratched her head and had all these little red marks on her hands and I asked her and she said, *fleas*. I can remember. She said, *fleas*. You left us with her. She had fleas. So did her parrot. You left. I remember I was really sad."

The radiator kicks in—the cat, emboldened by Peter's string beans, jumps onto the table and edges toward the cashew chicken. They have ordered from the place Grace insisted delivered something rancid to Mrs. Palowski though Maggie said nonsense, they have been ordering from there since before Grace was born. I'm not hungry anymore, she said before the food arrived.

"I don't think that parrot had fleas," Maggie says.

"It was flea ridden," Grace says. "A flea bag. A bag of fleas."

"Blimey!" Peter says.

"So, how is she?" Grace says.

"Who?" Maggie says.

"Aunt Mimi," Grace says.

"Aunt Mimi?" Maggie says.

"That's what she said. You don't remember? She said, 'Call me Aunt Mimi, as in Me-Me but with an *i-i*.' You laughed. You thought that was funny. I remember. You thought she was a riot, and you loved her parrot. You loved everything about her."

"I did?" Maggie says. "I said all that?"

How did the Obamas even meet? She's sure she's read it but now she can't recall. Is it important to the story? Is it important to the game? Maybe they met through Michelle's brother or that saintly mother. Perhaps families were involved, or mutual friends. They seem so perfect for one another—matching like two tall bookends: straight, learned, happy. She and Will met at a frat party: one of those orientation things. He sang with a band called the Urban Worms and wore glasses he called spectacles. He had a pink shirt ripped at the sleeves and a girlfriend back home he still loved or said he did. That summer they typed letters to one another they mailed back and forth. His parents ran an antiques business upstate and his brother smoked pot in a studio apartment in Columbus and he had an uncle and aunt nearby he visited for Sunday dinners of spaghetti and clams and as a kid he looked for arrowheads in the soybean fields when the fields were newly plowed. One night he showed her the collection he kept in a safe he brought to college, stones sharpened by stones into weapons. They lay in his narrow dorm bed and she said she thought the arrowheads in the shoe box looked like shards of graphite, and he said they don't grow soybeans anymore. I don't know what they grow anymore, he said.

But what was she saying again?

"Aunt Mimi's parrot," Grace says. She spritzes the cat from the cashew chicken and the cat jumps off the table, shivering. Grace has pulled away from her plate and sits more in front of the window, the setting sun piercing her skeletal shoulders, curved spine, sharp jaw. The translucence of her daughter's skin—ethereal, fading, the child for whom she and Will had waited so long disappearing. At Group many of the other girls appeared just this way, the hospital specializing in girls, their arms and legs thin as matchsticks, their heart rates fast as hummingbirds, their translucent skin—as if the organ intended to protect them had dissolved, or been scrubbed off by ED, the personified acronym.

Mrs. Palowski believed that part absurd, said Grace, the silly acronym for a deadly disease. Grace had returned to tell Mrs. Palowski all the poetic details: the weeks she spent in the room with an heiress from Houston who had been there three times before and was back and whose mother dated both a king and a prime minister, how the window, so high, looked out onto a dogwood with tiny pink blossoms, how one night it rained so hard and the lightning lit the room and in the morning the blossoms were entirely gone. Grounded, said the heiress.

But Maggie thought ED made perfect sense.

Is ED here? Maggie might ask her daughter now. She might grab Grace's crumbling shoulders and shake her. "Is ED in this fucking kitchen right now?" she might yell.

Let me tell you this, the Group leader had said. "ED is a sneaky asshole. He tells you you're ugly, you're fat. He's a misogynist who wants to control you. He does. You think about him day and night."

Maggie had listened as Will shifted in his seat to sneak a look at his phone. For this she will never forgive him.

"Flea bag," Grace says, turning to look at her—those eyes, truly gray, huge.

"Right. Fleabag," Maggie says. "Fleabag was still on her shoulder!"

"I don't buy it," Grace says.

"What do you mean?" Maggie says. "Parrots never die," she says. "They live forever. That's the thing. They are entirely devoted. They never go anywhere else. That parrot knew exactly everything—it knew me like yesterday."

"Nope," Grace says, aiming the spritz bottle at the window like a gun, taking a shot.

Someone shoves some trash down the chute; a phone rings in the upstairs apartment. Out the window the cirrus clouds have disappeared, replaced by a watery twilight. Cirrus clouds move at incredible speeds, Maggie happens to know. They might be halfway across the Atlantic or slicing through the moon.

Maggie should wipe off the dusty sill. She should change that faulty, flickering bulb. She should recaulk the tiles around the sink and throw out the old paper lantern, filthy, purge the cork bulletin board of its menus from restaurants long closed, party invitations, business cards, appointment cards, photographs of the kids as babies, artwork, notes, toss the spices she has never used from the pantry, the boxes of stale, half-unwrapped taco shells, the expired tins of beans, tomato sauce, and chicken stock. Somewhere there, in the recesses, on the floor, she stashed last year's Easter baskets with last year's plastic eggs, maybe a few forgotten chocolates and plastic grass, and here, on the white Formica table, she should gather the clutter of wrapped plastic utensils and chopsticks and shove them into the drawer already crammed so full it is difficult to open.

The all of it saved for, what? The day of the great picnic, they used to say when the kids were little-little. On the day of the great picnic, they said, we will need all the plastic forks and spoons, napkins, too. On the day of the great picnic, they said, we will make a huge paper napkin blanket and, just for fun, unwrap the chopsticks and build a chopstick tower to the sky, where the clouds will be not cirrus but the fluffy kind, cumulus, like on the ceiling of the Sistine Chapel, Michelangelo no fool; he painted the most beautiful clouds to be seen—clouds that meant better weather, clouds to float away on, clouds that hid angels and certain spirits too holy to ground, clouds tinged with a pink pigment of dried blood and crushed *statuario*, the white marble of Carrara. Crack it open, Michelangelo would say to the quarrymen, prisoners in dirty aprons, dust on their black trousers. Amaze me, he would say.

And they did. They amazed him, and the clouds will amaze you, they told the children, and the picnic will amaze you, they said, laid out on the huge paper napkin blanket underneath the chopstick tower—a feast: red grapes and Brie, strawberries dipped in chocolate, slices of turkey and roast beef and ham on thick baguettes, fried chicken, potato salad, chocolate chip cookies, cheesecake.

"I've got one," Grace says, still turned to the window, her shoulder blades wings picked clean.

"One what?" Maggie says.

"The game—I thought of my rose," she says.

"You did?" Maggie says. "Wow. That's fantastic,

that's great. Wonderful. Peter, did you hear? Grace has a rose!"

"Captain Flick," Peter says.

"Oh, for Chrissakes," Maggie says, pushing him off her lap. "Enough already."

"That *hurt*," Peter says, though Maggie barely hears him—she's turned to Grace, again, she's waiting on Grace, again, she's willing Grace, again, who may be gathering her thoughts or just counting heartbeats (please God, Maggie had said, passing all those starving girls in their rooms, some with tubes and others just staring at the ceiling, please God, she had prayed, please), her daughter's heart recalibrated, staccato, urgent.

"Tell me," Maggie says, taking Grace's cold hand, its bundle of bone and nerve. "Tell me."

DO SOMETHING

The soldiers keep Margaret in view. She carries her tripod, unsteadily, and an extra poncho for a bib. That they have let her come this far might be due to the weather, or possibly the kinds of amusements of which she remains unaware. Still, assume that they watch, tracking her as she stomps along the fence and positions herself by the sign that clearly states: NO TRESPASSING. GOVERNMENT PROPERTY. PHOTOGRAPHY FORBIDDEN.

It has turned a wet, wet September, everywhere raining so the leaves, black and slick, paste to the soles of her boots, or Caroline's: Wellingtons borrowed from the back of the hallway closet where earlier Harry watched as Margaret rummaged, wondering where she could possibly be going in such weather.

She turned, boot in hand.

"It's raining," he repeated.

Deaf at most decibels, Harry now cast his voice into the silence, as if hoping for an echo or a nod.

"Nowhere," she had said, because this is nowhere, or anywhere, or somewhere not particularly known: an hour's drive from Wilmington if you took the busy roads, and then country, mostly, the drizzle graying the already gray landscape. Ye olde et cetera—cornfields, silos, a ravaged billboard for

Daniel's peas, fresh from California, though this is technically Delaware and the land of soybeans. Ducks, too, the fall season in full swing; the drizzle split by the crack crack crack of the hunters' guns.

She parked near the drainage ditch that edges the fence, chain link, as if for dogs, though there are no dogs here, only a guard tower, a landing field, and the soldiers who wait for the planes. But that isn't right, exactly. The place is vast, a city of a place, with barracks—are those called barracks?—and trucks and cul-de-sacs and no doubt children sleeping, Army brats—or is this Marines?—in the two-story housing labyrinth not so far from where she gets out, near the drainage ditch, near the landing field, near the place where the plane will descend. This she knows. The rest—the presence of children, the numbers involved, the ranking, the hierarchy—she truthfully has no idea.

Margaret skewers the tripod in the mud and adjusts the poncho to cover her. Today, she plans to bite skin. She can almost taste it: the salt of it, the flesh; see herself in her resistance: Margaret Morrisey, mother to Caroline and the dead one, James; wife to Harry. She mounts the camera on the track and angles the lens toward where the plane will descend—they come from the east, she has learned, out of Mecca, the bodies mostly wrapped in flags but sometimes carried in a tiny box.

"Christ, Mother," Caroline said after the first arrest, the fine. "Get a life."

"Your great-great-grandfather ate horse feed; that was his dinner. He'd soften the oats with spit. He came to this country for food. Literally."

"Apropos of . . . ?" Caroline said.

"It meant something," Margaret said. "America."

"It's illegal."

"This is a free country."

"Please," Caroline said.

The two sat at Caroline's kitchen table, Caroline in one of her suits meant for business, her cigarette burning in the misshapen ashtray a ten-year-old James had spun out of clay. Caroline's children were elsewhere, having reached the age of the disappeared—their voices shouting orders from behind the locked doors of their bedrooms or even standing present, their bodies imperfect, studded casts of their former selves; if they were somewhere within them they were very, very deep.

"I should never have told you I voted for him," Caroline said.

"I would have guessed."

"The rules have to do with respect," Caroline said. "Or something. Anyway, they're the rules. It's law. Besides, it's none of our business. None of your business."

"Says whom?" Margaret said, to which Caroline had some sort of reply.

Margaret listened for a while, and then she did not; she thought of other things, how she would like to have believed that not so long ago Caroline would have stood beside her at the fence, that her daughter would have carried a sign or at least shouted an obscenity. But this was before Caroline took that job in the Financial District. The Fucked District, she calls it, but the money's good, she says. It's serious money.

"Mother?"

"I was listening," Margaret said.

"Forget it," Caroline said. She tapped her nails, those nails, on the table, then the buzzer rang—delivery—and the conversation ended.

"Dinnertime," she yelled in the direction of the doors.

Crack. Crack. Crack.

The men have had enough. They climb down from their tower to slog through duck country, technically Delaware, the first state, though most have trouble with the history; one can hear their boots, or is that frogs? The sucking. Soon enough they'll reach her. Margaret records their magnified approach; records them unlocking the gate and stepping to the other side, records their blank expressions. The trouble is she can only pretend to hate them.

"Good morning, Mrs. Morrisey." This from the one Margaret calls Tweedledee.

She straightens up, adjusts the poncho.

"We'll remind you that you're trespassing. That taking photographs is forbidden."

"Today," she says, hand on tripod, "I plan to resist."

Their arms remain folded. Four pair, as usual; a pack; a team; a unit, perhaps; or would they be a regiment? No, a regiment is bigger, a regiment is many. She tries to remember from soldier days, from mornings James explained the exact order of things—sergeant to lieutenant to captain to king—his miniature warriors arranged throughout the house in oddly purposeful groupings. She would find them everywhere, assaulting a sock, scaling the Ping-Pong table, plastic, molded men with clearly defined weaponry and indistinct faces. When she banished them to his room, fearing someone would break a neck, James had cried and cried.

"That would be more than your usual fine, Mrs. Morrisey."

He is a horse's ass, but then again, a boy once James's age who should be pitied.

"I plan to resist," she repeats. One of the Mute Ones has his hand out as if to help her across the muddy plain. They are waiting, she knows, for Margaret to do something. Collapse, she thinks, then does, more a buckle than a collapse, knowing full well the ridiculousness of it, how small she'll become. The big one bends down to help her. Now, she thinks, though it is not until it is done that she understands she has found the courage to do it, biting the soft part of that hand, the hammock of skin between thumb and forefinger.

Caroline sits next to Harry in the detention waiting room (she must have taken the train!), no question who's the boss. Our girl could split atoms, Harry once said. We ought to lease her to GE.

Sorry, darling, Margaret mouths to him. He looks at her with his doggy yellow eyes; then Caroline leads them both out.

In the sunshine they blink: "Look at the weather!" Margaret says, reflexively. "What a treat!"

Caroline has opened the car door.

"Get in," she says.

They sit in silence to home, the radio punched to static and static and static then punched off, again, then the familiar drive, the front door, the hallway, the kitchen. Caroline makes tea and calls a Family Meeting. There's a hole in the place where James would have been so Margaret steps in and wanders around while Caroline speaks of Responsibility and Reputation and Appropriate Behavior, and, yes, the Germs in Your Mouth, and Patriotism, but mostly, mostly, mostly, Mother, Embarrassment.

"Please," Caroline says. "I'm at wit's end."

Margaret would like to cradle Caroline in her arms, Caroline sleepy and hatted and a bit jaundice yellow, but she cannot. Caroline has grown; she's taller than Margaret and twice divorced and a millionaire, she has confessed. A mill-ion-aire, she said.

"Where are your friends, Mother?" Caroline asks.

Margaret shrugs. She hasn't thought of friends recently, or her standing Wednesday at Sheer Perfection; her hair's gone shaggy and gray and her cuticles have grown over their moons.

"I'm sorry, darling," she says. "I'll stop."

How has it come to this? There was Youth, Margaret thinks. Then, Love: a certain indefatigable, copper-colored Spirit. Wasn't she the one who had convinced Harry to do a U-turn on the GW Bridge? And what of Leonard Nan's retirement? She'd worn a blond wig and pharmaceutical pearls, hula-hooped her toast gyrating the thing to her knees. She used to leave it all to chance, or Certain Men, actually. Wasn't she the one with the Robert Kennedy dartboard? Didn't she support Nixon to the finish?

Now she is blindsided by fury; the tide of her anger rising at certain unpredictable moments (yes, the *tide*), as if drawn by an internal moon, waxing and waning, though mostly waning.

A disclaimer, first: she lost no one in the Tragedy,

no Hero her James, just an ordinary mortal, his (by inference) an unheroic death: cancer of the blood—blah blah blah—one cell fried—blah—and then another—blah blah—until nothing remained but bone and sinew, James's lungs mechanically pumping, a ring of them singing before they turned off the machine. Godspeed. And the machine stopped. Godspeed. Which is not to say she didn't know someone who knew someone; which is not to say she forgets we are living under the Cloud of It, that there are Reliable Threats, that Evil Lurks, that there are those who seek to undermine our Way of Life.

Yet if asked she will say James's death was her 9/11.

"We all have our very own," she'll say. "Don't you agree?"

Crack. Crack. Crack.

The next time Tweedledee steps away from the others, approaching alone, the Big One with the bandaged hand hanging back as if on lookout.

"Did it hurt?" she calls to him. "Am I toxic? Infectious?"

"I'll ask you to read the sign, Mrs. Morrisey," says Tweedledee.

"It's a free country," Margaret says.

"Not exactly," he says. Clearly there's a manual on How to Speak to the Protesters and/or the Criminally Insane.

"I'm not interested in the bodies," she says. "It's the wildlife I'm after."

"Camera's forbidden," he says.

He stands, square and sharp against the autumnal reds, his camouflage humorless, stuck in the sole season of winter. If she could see his eyes she predicts she would see embarrassment there, but they remain mirrored lenses, and anyway she is wrong: he is doing his job.

"Glorious day," she says, but he doesn't bite.

"So you can shoot them but you can't photograph them? I find that ridiculous. Ridiculous," she calls out to the Big One. "Does it still hurt?"

She grips the camera with her dirty fingers, though it is looped around her neck and going nowhere.

"You're trespassing, Mrs. Morrisey. This is Government Property."

She plunks down in Tweedledee's shadow, her arms crossed.

"In Sweden there's no such thing," she says, squinting up. "You can camp anywhere. It's allowed. You could take a walk across the entire country if you wanted and no one could say, private property. I'd call that democracy, wouldn't you?"

He looms over her like a man mountain—trees and shrubs the pattern—his mirrored glasses the stone at the top, the place of the vista that from a distance could be snow, or water; bright, regardless, in the glaring sun. She waits as he gestures to the Mute Ones, to the Big One with the bandaged hand. They are all tired of her, it's clear, and bored. They step forward, unlocking their handcuffs, clicking and unclicking as if they'd rather be elsewhere. Even Tweedledee wipes his forehead in an exhausted, parched gesture. She thinks of how he sees himself now, how he pictures himself—soldier or statesman— protecting the all of us from God knows what: nothing; everything: an old woman with a camera. He protects is all, he's like a postage stamp or a flag; a symbol bought and sold, something with an adhesive strip to stick on an automobile bumper or football helmet—thirty-seven cents or a dollar ten in the big bin at Rite Aid.

The handcuffs are tighter than she would have imagined, and she finds herself humming the only song she can think to hum: "Amazing Grace," knowing, even while humming, how ridiculous she sounds, how outdated it's become, even quaint: peace. She thinks to mention this to Caroline, to somehow explain: What she is trying to do is to aim for something real, she'll tell her, something that is not just an approximation of real.

Here the two of us, she'll say, the all of us: the soldiers, the protester, were all from a scene already enacted; so that even my own inclination to *be*—

Caroline interrupts. "To what?"

The fine has already been paid, though this time they fingerprinted—"Ma'am," Tweedledee had said to Caroline. "Tell your mother to keep her mouth shut."

Be, Margaret says now. "To *be.*"

"Or not," says the Millionaire.

"When did everything stop being real?" Margaret says.

"Don't bring James into it."

"He would have—"

Caroline plugs her ears; she might be eight again: a girl in braids and kneesocks, six missing teeth so that she could no more blow a bubble than recite Pope, though James, a teacher at heart, had tried for weeks.

"I don't care, Mother. I mean, I do, but at some point you have to put yourself first."

"Like hell."

"What?" Caroline unplugs her ears.

"I said, I know."

"You know what?"

"I know you don't care."

The bubble burst, the lopsided attempt. James picked it himself out of Caroline's braids, though Margaret had still given him a scolding and threatened the back side of the hairbrush. James put it all in his Feelings Jar, a jar that, in its earlier life, contained dill pickles.

I was just trying to DO SOMETHING. I was

just trying to teach her how to blow bubbles and you got so mad you could spit.

"I am just trying to Do Something," Margaret says, though Caroline is busy looking for dinner inspiration, for anything other than pasta. "You don't care to understand. It's like everything. Conversation, for example, is now just approximations of opinions adopted from other opinions that were approximations of opinions, et cetera, et cetera. I'm just trying to be real when everything is an approximation."

But this is not true, exactly. Death is not an approximation. It is completely real; it is unchangeable, forever—an approximation of nothing. Hadn't she seen it that first time she'd found the base, the barracks, the military galaxy? Where had she been going? She can't remember anymore. She was lost, she knew, had taken to driving, punching the radio to listen to men and women discussing God knows what, anything to drown out her own inside voice. Use your inside voice, she used to tell the children, meaning quiet. Softly. Hers shouted now; tore its hair.

She had followed the convoy of jeeps, had stopped across the highway with the other cars, curious at the rows and rows of them idling like so many school buses by the chain-link fence that surrounded the complex of guard towers and apartments and houses and a post office there in the middle of nowhere, or everywhere: soybean

242

fields, corn crops, a V of geese heading south, and somewhere else, just beyond, an abandoned barn where starlings roost in rotted eaves and a boy necks or smokes or pings his pocketful of stones one by one against the glass, wanting breakage: all boys do. At the center sat the plane, exceedingly complicated, wings folded and a scissored tail—more like a jackknife than anything that could fly—and from it soldiers transporting bodies, their families there to receive them, to take them back as real, as dead.

"This is no approximation," Margaret says. "This is what that idiot has the audacity to hide: the one thing true in the mess of it," she says, attempting to name it all for Caroline, who some time ago surrendered, running the sauce jar under hot water, her back to Margaret though presumably listening.

Now she turns, her hand dripping.

"I hear you, Mother," she says, popping the lid; she forks a noodle from the boiling pot and holds it out to Margaret. "Finito?" she asks.

Margaret dreams of James. In this one he steps out of the Cape Cod surf (those were the years!) wet and gleaming; he is as he was, a young man, a boy who loved books, who copied passages in letters to his mother, certain things he believed she might like, understanding her taste, he once wrote, in these matters.

Dear Mother, his name is Professor Burns, which is ironic, because he smokes like a chimney and even when not keeps the cigarette, somehow lit, behind his ear. There's a rumor his hair once caught on fire and he lost his place in his notes and for the rest of the semester kept one step ahead of the syllabus oblivious. He is a little odd, but I like him and this is my favorite class. I don't know if I love poetry or just love the way he talks about poetry. I don't know if I just love that anyone can talk about poetry at all how many years later and still weep. Yes, he weeps. Or did the other day after his lecture on Byron. A few of the girls went up to console him; maybe it was just a ploy (ha-ha).

Here he is! Margaret thinks in her dream. Look, here he is! He's been swimming—that scamp—all along!

She hears the waves roll out behind him, the crash of it so clearly. She is fearful he might decide to return to that riptide; how often has she warned him it could carry you for miles! But, no. He walks toward her, the sun behind him dazzling. He is a perfect boy, a young man of promise without a single broken bone, nothing to be mended, stitched; strong-hearted. He takes no medications, she could tell you, and on that repeatedly filled-out form that has so many boxes in which to check yes he checks no, no, no, no! every time. He is no more an approximation than a red tulip in May, and here is the great joke of it: He is Real!

A delicious pain, almost sexual, wakes her. It is the great cruel trick of the night: to wake alone, regardless. She can scream or cry if she wants— Caroline's gone home, and Harry is deaf asleep. She elbow-props herself to watch him breathe, he the father of her children, the great love of her life. He floats into outer space in his bubble. It will burst, eventually, and he, like the rest of them, will be gone.

To where?

An approximation of this, perhaps, or the curl of a shell, the color of leaves, a gesture; here but somewhere deep within.

James had once asked her what she believed; this toward the end of him, she remembers, or close enough. And she might have lied; she might have given her boy something more.

"Nothing," she had said, already furious. "Absolutely nothing."

He sat in the chair by the window. She had brought a blue shawl and oatmeal cookies she would set by the door for visitors.

"You're an original, Mom. I've meant to tell you," he said.

"Thank you, darling," she said, wanting to hear more and wanting him to stop. She stood by the edge of his bed; she liked to stand there. She even liked this room, or well enough, on the quiet floor, with its view over the low rooftops to the sliver of river when the light went right, which happened more often now, in this season. It had been autumn; the sun low, at a slant. That she found it too difficult to look at him she couldn't explain.

"And I forgive you your trespasses," he said.

"Hallelujah," she said.

If she had looked she would have noticed the blueness of the shawl, how odd to see him wrapped in blue.

"I hope you're wrong," he said.

"It wouldn't be the first time."

"If you are, I'll come back and rattle the windows," he said. "Think of it as my 'so there.'"

The windows more than rattle; so there. The wind more than blows. And somewhere else the terrified children must listen for what else—the cavalry, the infantry, the artillery—what had James taught her? Nothing. Everything. The names run together to a pooled point, the way blood will when the heart stops beating, when the machine stops. The machine stopped.

That she gets out of bed and dresses is almost beside the point. She no longer needs to write a note. She throws on loose clothing and goes, forgetting her empty camera—It was just like in the movies! she told Caroline. The soldiers rolled out the film and flung it in the garbage! They called her bite his wound!—forgetting her purse, backing the station wagon out the long drive to swerve down the once-dirt road toward the highway. At this hour there's little traffic, and she can speed as much as she likes, the cornfields and rows of soybeans saluting as she passes; in the end her only ally, the landscape, the actual black dirt of the country. Government property, my ass, she thinks.

Her headlights flood the woods she turns in to: wild, brush grown, skunk cabbage in the hollows and arrowheads to be found; the all of it disturbed by this strange, Halloween wind. There might be children behind the trees, trick-or-treaters, Frankensteins and ghosts and ghouls shaking the skinny limbs of the aspen saying, I'm here! No, here! But they'd be flushed out, of course, by her, by the klieg lights on the landing field: in case of emergencies, no doubt: the jackknife slicing the air into ribbons, the families the only witness to the dead.

And what had she planned, anyway? To whom would she have shown her pictures? Harry? Caroline? Absent friends?

She parks near the guard tower and slams the door. The steel latticework seems to glow in the moonlight, rising to the little booth of their tree-house watch. She might see breath on the glass, it is that cold and not so far up, or frost; she knows he is in there and she could find him if she climbed.

When did it become the boy she is after?

Does a radio play? Does he write a letter home?

She wants to know where he's from, what he studied in school. She's interested in his early artwork, she could tell him. Elementary. Preschool, even. Did he begin with circles? Those circles! And then slowly, no; she had seen it in her children and her children's friends and her grandchildren, even. The loss of circles, eventually. Don't despair, she could tell him. It happens to everyone.

She would like to know where he sat in the cafeteria—with the popular children or off a little by himself, like her James, his sandwich crushed from his book bag, a tuna fish on white bread or maybe peanut butter. Did his mother include notes? An *I love you,* or *Hi, Handsome!* Perhaps he was not a son who required encouragement; perhaps he did fine on his own. His were not elaborate tastes—she can guess this—nor particularly demanding. He seemed fine with what he got until he wasn't; and when he wasn't he didn't complain. He made plans—how to leave, how to get out, how to make do, survive.

Was he interested in trains? Did he play a musical instrument?

Margaret stands at the fence looking in. The worst thing, she would tell him, is that she can no longer distinguish stars; when I think I have found one it moves out of view, just metal in orbit or a transportation vehicle. There are no longer fixed points by which to determine my direction, she would tell him. How can I ever again make a wish?

You are not responsible, she would say. It is shameful what we've done to you. We should all of us be ashamed.

"You are just like the rest of us," she says. "You are only trying to Do Something."

Does Margaret shout this or whisper? It no longer matters. She is suddenly tired and aware that she should go. She'll return home the way she came, driving back through ye olde et cetera to her rightful place beside Harry: Margaret Morrisey, mother to Caroline and the dead one, James.

Hormones, she'll tell Caroline, by way of explanation.

I miss him, too, Caroline will say, by way of apology.

"Goodbye," Margaret calls to them, though none can hear for the crack crack crack; the hunters particularly ravenous at dawn.

RADICAL
FEMINISTS

Beatrice Wells is on her way to Bryant Park with her boys, ice-skating, Saturday afternoon, when she bumps, literally, into Jonathan Fontaine, his hair, though thinner, still as his name would suggest, puffed, coiffed, as if Jonathan Fontaine has just stepped out of a zany French farce. She's grazed his hand with the rusty blade of her ice skate—it's been forever since she's used them, high school, when she would go with friends to Crowfield to play crack the whip, she the lightest, the most daring, the first one to be spun out, to go the farthest, flung—and there's blood. She dabs at it with a snotty Kleenex she finds shredded in the pocket of her parka, apologizing and apologizing as Jonathan Fontaine stands with his limp hand in hers; she forgets who she's tending for a moment and spits on the Kleenex to rub harder.

"Gross," Charlie, her older son, says. "That's disgusting, Mom."

"It's all right," Jonathan Fontaine says, by way of reprimand. "Your mother and I go way back," he adds, and something about the way he says it makes Beatrice want to cry, and so she does, secretly, using the other half of the shredded Kleenex for herself.

The day has turned warm, too warm for late December. Throngs of desperate shoppers swarm the scarves, the tiny glass animals, the candles they don't need nor would anyone else want at the dozens of outdoor holiday kiosks encircling Bryant Park. Within them skaters glide over the frozen pond, assembled a few months earlier by Santa's elves and open to the public free of charge, as Louis Armstrong and Ella Fitzgerald sing a jaunty duet from speakers camouflaged among the bare sycamores, the trees' gray limbs garlanded with Christmas lights and electrical cords and deflated, errant balloons. Tourists mingle and watch, hoping to report New York back home—detachment, concentration, angst—like the guy who skates alone in the center of the rink, his fur vest of unknown animal origin, his hands scissoring the air like beaks, his stretchy black tights, his balls two grapes on a plucked stem. Near him girls fresh from the American Girl Place with Kit, the child of the Depression, or Tabitha, child of the civil rights movement, or Esmeralda, child of Cuban immigrants, clutched in their arms balance and glide on wobbly ankles, delighted with their dolls' hair, newly set at the store's beauty salon, their dolls strapped into tiny chairs as women wearing white lab coats and surgeons' gloves tugged at the accumulated knots of too much girl attention, too much girl love. Now they all beam out, organized.

"Please," Jonathan Fontaine is saying, the wind tousling. "A flesh wound. I'll live."

"So funny, of all people," Beatrice says, looking up at him. The two stand across from one another, fairly close, Beatrice's boys leaning in hip to hip.

"Boys," Beatrice remembers. "This is Jonathan. Mr. Fontaine."

Jonathan Fontaine reaches to shake Charlie's hand, and then Sam's. He is a slight man, not much taller than either of her sons: they could take him down, she thinks, imagining it: Jonathan Fontaine impeccably dressed—some fashionable well-cut coat and a bright red scarf purchased at Barneys or Saks, the color, if a shade or two higher, of his flushed cheeks— wrestled to the gravelly path, pinned on his back. The boys rightly sense he has no children or any understanding of their language and customs; they will last three minutes tops before pulling at Beatrice's arms, before spying one of the outdoor Ping-Pong tables and begging to play. Go ahead, Beatrice will say to them. Don't kill your brother, Beatrice will add to Charlie. Five minutes, Beatrice will call, watching as her boys hurry away.

In the years since Beatrice Wells worked for Jonathan Fontaine, she has often pictured bumping into him, though never literally. For

255

a while, she would most often imagine sitting across from him in court, Jonathan Fontaine dressed for the role, gray suit, spiffy tie, shiny loafers if one were to strip the witness stand and see. The judge listens to the charge with a look on her face. This is nothing she hasn't heard before, or experienced firsthand herself. She's already bored with how predictable it all is— didn't she sign on for more exciting complaints? Who cares? This is news?

In the fantasy Beatrice Wells's lawyer is trim. A professional who runs marathons on weekends, her hair pulled back in a sleek ponytail, her stockings stretched taut over her muscular calves. If you looked in her refrigerator you'd find only blueberries and Greek yogurt, several bottles of white wine. She stands before Jonathan Fontaine and raises a shaky fist. Unlike the judge, she is paid to care, so now the jury, eleven women and one old man who usually snores so loudly the court stenographer has to stop the proceedings, listens rapt with attention.

"Would you say, Mr. Fontaine, that you *intimidated* Ms. Wells?" the lawyer asks.

"She's a big girl," Jonathan Fontaine says. In the overheated courtroom he wears a cashmere V-neck under his suit jacket. If he crossed his legs in a certain way, you'd see his silk socks slipped down, his hairless legs, white as veal.

"And you noticed?"

"Of course I noticed! Who wouldn't?" he says. "So she's female, case closed. There are certain considerations when working with the Y chromosome, certain considerations that should be addressed head-on, no pun intended. I don't go in for subtleties."

"So you're saying you admit you saw her first as a woman," the lawyer says.

"First. Second. Third."

"And you took note?"

"With pleasure," Jonathan Fontaine says, winking at the lawyer, leaning in. "Are you male-identified, Ms. . . . ?"

"Esquire," the lawyer says.

"So you hear me."

"I'm comfortable with both sexes," the lawyer says.

"So you're bi-identified."

"Let's just say I assume the proper position for either situation."

"Missionary?" Jonathan Fontaine says.

"Objection!" This protest, surprisingly, from Beatrice Wells, who rarely spoke in her own fantasies but rather watched as other, more powerful women spoke for her. "I requested someone sympathetic! I requested someone who would *get* it!"

"Oh, I *get* it," the lawyer says, turning toward Beatrice, who sees, for the first time, that the lawyer is herself.

• • •

"Beatrice?" Jonathan Fontaine is saying; he's apparently been speaking.

"Oh," Beatrice says. "Right. Freelance, mostly. Teaching from time to time. Hunter. City College. You can usually land something."

"And you never went back?"

"Hah. Well. Until a few years ago, it was all I could do to wear a shirt right side out," Beatrice says.

"They're beautiful boys," Jonathan Fontaine says.

"Yes, they are," Beatrice says, watching them smack a Ping-Pong ball back and forth, the attendant hovering as if convinced they will break something, and they will; they always do. In her fantasy of this meeting, her sons would have sat down at a chess table, easily beating the old chess masters who normally milked tourists, smacking their hands on the timers before the tourists had a chance to think. The boys would have won; the old chess masters would have eaten their hats.

"You?" she says, turning back to him. They both know it's a rhetorical question.

"The usual insanity," Jonathan Fontaine says. "Davos. TED. I'll be in Beijing tomorrow, the summit on the Future of Our World. You know. Invitational. I'm here for a hostess gift." He looks out toward the jumble of kiosks. "She's into cats, apparently."

Jonathan Fontaine's breath is a cloud, his eyes a watery blue, blank. He turns back to her. "Any ideas?" he says, then looks off into the mid-distance, as if trying to conjure a more interesting audience, or at the very least, a more populous one. She wouldn't say he'd aged so much as hardened, or rather, settled into himself, like a sedimentary rock; in a cross slice she could find the evolution of Jonathan Fontaine— precious youth, adored son, educated at one of those ancient institutions where the boys put on Shakespeare and adopt all the parts, their fairest Desdemona waving his handkerchief from the top of the wooden staircase, its railing polished by the sweaty, masturbatory hands of his thousands of predecessors, the fathers and grandfathers and great-grandfathers of same; from there somewhere better, the highlight of which a coveted invitation to join his master at high table, his master instructing him in all things male—the donning of the black cloak and hat, the patience to wait for the gong announcing their procession and ascension to the stage. (Now ten men here to every woman, though in the master's day none were permitted, he'd explain, recounting again the infamous story of the Girton girl who dressed up as a boy and was caught—they were always caught. She's been asked to leave the college— true story—and now she's married to the great Hudgins in Philosophy but still she won't show up. You'd think she'd get over it.) From there New York, where he'd begun as an editorial assistant and ascended to publisher by the time Beatrice Wells came into his life, an illustrator, an artist, the front-runner to head the graphics department.

And what of the evolution of Beatrice Wells? Precocious youth, adored daughter, educated at one of those ancient institutions where the girls performed Shakespeare and took on all the roles, Macduff shouting down from the top of the wooden staircase, the wooden banister polished by the powdered palms of their mothers and grandmothers and great-grandmothers, three of whom had founded the school on the second floor of a brownstone, their names inscribed in the keystone of the recently opened state-of-the-art building that housed the music rooms and the media rooms and the language rooms and the science labs and the art studios. Here the girls were taught by a faculty culled from the best schools east of the Mississippi—nothing they didn't know. Ask us! they would say at assembly. Seek us out! Question us! Demand of us!

Every Friday morning their leader, Dr. Frances Pearlman, in black polyester pants and sturdy shoes, limped to the podium and cleared her throat to read a poem by some forgotten poetess, or a quote from a woman no one has ever heard of—Hannah Whitall Smith or Mary Winsor—

insisting they commit it all to memory, or at the very least, write it down in their assembly books. Photographs of girls in white blouses and pleated skirts, shoulder to shoulder, arranged by height, positioned to be seen—class of 1918, class of 1937, class of 1951, class of 1972— kept sentinel as the girls listened to Dr. Pearlman drone on and on, as the girls spooned dry cereal into their mouths, stirred more brown sugar into their oatmeal, knowing they could copy whatever it was they were supposed to be remembering from Winifred Titlebaum, who groveled, per usual, at Dr. Pearlman's feet. Afterward, during her morning free period, Beatrice sketched in the glorious art studio, its floor-to-ceiling windows donated by an alumna, Mary Beth Howard, so that more girls, she had said, her voice quivery with emotion at the groundbreaking, her tight gray curls capped by an ill-becoming hard hat, could be "brought into the light." Beatrice's drawings were beautiful amalgams of the life studies model, her imagination, and a vague understanding of the artistic temperament— gleaned from the fifth-form requirement the Fall of the Romantics, with particular attention to Shelley's *Frankenstein* and the life of Mary Wollstonecraft—drawings that paved her way to art school, where she smoked and drank with the best of them. From there she moved to New York, renting a one-bedroom on Grove Street with a wisteria snaking up the building's brick facade, painting in the mornings and waiting tables in the evenings, before landing a job in the graphics department. Throughout it all there were times when she caught herself holding her breath for the thing that had been promised her to finally happen. It would, she knew, it would.

But this is all off subject.

The subject is Beatrice Wells and Jonathan Fontaine, an abrupt meeting on a windy, warmish, late December afternoon in New York, between Fifth and Sixth off Forty-second Street, Bryant Park. Picture them bumping into one another as strangers often do in New York, especially in December, especially in midtown, where at this time of year a surge of bepackaged tourists converges with the usual businessmen and businesswomen, bike messengers, street hawkers, commuters, pickpockets, actors, beggars, shoe shiners, and now ice skaters, given that the pond has magically appeared, the city's troubadours revived. (This, the first time she's been in the neighborhood for ages, she had said. She had to twist the boys' arms, to practically drag them!) The two had jostled for a moment before recognizing one another, before realizing that they were familiar, somehow, though it had been many years since Beatrice Wells had screwed her courage to the sticking place and knocked on the door, ajar, of Jonathan Fontaine's large office, his collection of antique typewriters lining the one uncluttered shelf against the back wall, the view out his double-hung window of a quaint, lost New York: dirty, honky-tonk, flashy, like something now on HBO.

She had entered with ease, her oversize portfolio, somewhat a formality, tucked under her arm; she felt confident, happy, completely qualified or even, over: at this point she could have performed the job eyes closed, she could have sat in Jonathan Fontaine's place, even, her feet on his desk. She had just that morning performed a ritual, of sorts, rereading the accumulated wisdom of generations in her Assembly book, the snippets and bon mots relayed by Dr. Pearlman on those dreary Friday mornings, the girls gathered in their Lanz nightgowns and furry slippers, dried egg whites on their faces from makeovers the night before; she had even shared a few with her husband, a public relations man, an old flame from art school, another story. "Wish me luck," she'd said to him.

"Attagirl," he'd answered—he'd been raised by missionaries in Minnesota so she was used to this—"hear me roar," he'd said, smiling at her in the mirror, half his face white with shaving foam.

Now she listens as Jonathan Fontaine explains how the typewriters were purchased at a recently defunct store in New Haven, a city where he'd spend a year or two perfecting his drinking skills at Mory's. This one, he says, pointing to a dark black machine with small round keys, the gold-leafed letters looking as if they'd been individually painted with a single-haired brush, belonged to S. R. Hutchison. On this baby he wrote his *Universal Survey of Art*, volumes one through six, and here, he says, moving on to a heavier looking one, its keys raised so high you might imagine the user needed to stand, A. H. Heider composed *On the Migrations of Seven Continents*, or rather his wife, the long-suffering Melanie, typed its fourteen drafts.

"The accumulated wisdom of generations," Jonathan Fontaine says, his hand in a sweep. "I've been at it since my undergraduate days," he says. "You?"

"Me?" Beatrice says.

"Are you a collector?"

"Not particularly," Beatrice says, thinking she should have come up with something: silver spoons, first editions, a Curran purchased for pennies from a gallery in the East Village.

"Please," Jonathan Fontaine says, pushing a heavy book off a small chair in front of his desk. "Have a seat."

"Thank you," Beatrice says. She can feel her heart pounding, the color rising, why? She's a thirty-two-year-old woman, a professional, and besides, it's only Jonathan Fontaine, twenty years, give or take, her senior: she's been here long enough, he knows her worth. And still, and still, he sits across from her, the big boss, his blue eyes steady, his thicket of hair fluffed as if by a blast of air. If she could crawl into its hiding place and put her ear to his skull, what would she hear? No doubt the thinking of Jonathan Fontaine's elaborately coddled brain, the revolutions of his well-oiled wheel of judgment, his consideration as he stares at Beatrice Wells, bright by all accounts and more than qualified, her bow tie perky, a nice touch.

Jonathan Fontaine smiles. "Everyone's impressed with what you've done around here."

"Thank you," Beatrice says. "That's nice," she says.

"And now the senior position? How so?" he asks, leaning back, crossing his legs, his hands on his knee, and though she's momentarily stuck by the awkward construction of the question, Beatrice soon regains her bearings and launches forth—gaining, as she goes, a building momentum, an ease. She spins farther and farther from the question, flying, flung, explaining to Jonathan Fontaine how as a child she had filled countless sketchbooks, read the journals of René Robert Bouché and the great George Barbier, studied the Exposition Universelle of 1889, the construction of the Eiffel Tower and Berlin in the Roaring Twenties, the works of Marie Laurencin, Grandma Moses, et cetera, et cetera, how she'd briefly—he'd seen in her résumé, which he now held loosely, reviewing—worked toward a graduate degree at NYU but soon found hers was not a spirit suited for academia, its backbiting, its ennui, hers a spirit suited for this, for here, for exactly what he offered, what she wanted, what she'd worked toward, what she'd dreamed of: truly. Breathless, or rather, spent, Beatrice abruptly sits on her hands as Jonathan Fontaine seems to, for the second or third time, drift off.

"Delighted," he says, to no one in particular. "First rate," he says. "Now," he says. "A few questions." He leans forward again, the keys from T. R. Peterson's ancient Smith-Corona visible just over his left shoulder, poised as if anticipating Peterson's brilliant ghost. "You're married, right? Recently?"

"Four months," Beatrice says. "June third," she says, wondering how they got here and where they are going.

Jonathan Fontaine nods then stretches and takes off his suit jacket; she notices the neatly folded handkerchief in his pocket: a nice touch.

"Congratulations," he says.

"Oh, well. We've been living together for ages," Beatrice says. Outside, music flares from the opened sash of the double-hung window— the break-dancing decade long passed, though in neighborhoods like this one "Thriller" won't die.

"Now, I could get sued for this," Jonathan Fontaine says, pausing, smiling again. She sees a bit of spit on a tooth, the sparkle of it, and notices the delicacy of his features, his eyebrows so fair as to be almost disappeared. "But you're not planning on getting pregnant anytime soon," he says. "Are you?"

Beatrice sits back in her small chair. "What?" she says. She's stalling, of course; she's heard every word.

"Pregnant," Jonathan Fontaine says. He stands and shuts the window, the noise ineffectively gagged. "We need someone to hit the ground running," he says, sitting back down, picking up a paper clip. "You understand the issue with mothers," he says, bending the paper clip. "Birthday parties. Trips to the dentist. That sort of thing."

"Oh, God, yes," Beatrice says. "I mean, no. I mean, I understand, but God, no." They had been trying since their trip to city hall, calling it their Paris years: sex in the afternoon—in the shower, sometimes, on the moldy living room couch; sex in the evening; sex in the morning, the wisteria budding, fading, drying, its smell so faint, just a whiff from time to time, on the pillows. No interruption for *le petit chapeau*, just straight start to finish, glorious; she might, at this moment, be hosting a burrowing sperm, or thousands of them; at this precise moment one of her tiny eggs, still springy, might be rent in two. Now she leans forward, conspiratorial.

"No," she says. "Never."

When Beatrice Wells called her husband from the street corner to tell him what her boss, the asshole Jonathan Fontaine, had said to her, her husband would not believe her. "He didn't mean that," he said. "He must have meant something else," he said.

"What?" she said. "What else could he have possibly meant?"

"Not that," her husband said.

"See, that's the problem. Right there," she said. "Nobody ever wants to believe us. Nobody. Not even women," she said. "Not even women want to believe women. Look at Anita Hill and Phyllis Schlafly."

"You're overreacting," he said.

"I could sue him," Beatrice said.

"You could," her husband said.

"I would lose," Beatrice said.

"You would," her husband said.

"I mean, it's none of his business, none of his goddamn business," Beatrice said.

"It's not," her husband said.

"Our bodies, ourselves," Beatrice said, somewhat inexplicably.

"Ditto," her husband said, equally so.

Jonathan Fontaine doesn't want to spend more than thirty dollars but he needs something presentable, he says. Unique. He is hopeless at these things, as she might imagine, all thumbs, and he remembers she had a good eye, an excellent eye. He pulls his coat tighter, the wound, or rather, scratch exposed on his hand. Beyond them the boys are in the grips of a Ping-Pong tournament with what appear to be two hustlers; some holiday shoppers warm their hands on hot cocoa or cider and watch; the sun slips behind Times Square and the day gets predictably dark and colder. Louis Armstrong and Ella Fitzgerald seem oblivious to it all. "I guess she really doesn't want to dance," Beatrice says—the song on what seems like an endless loop.

"Sorry?" Jonathan Fontaine says.

"Okay," Beatrice says. "I'd be happy to," she says.

In the court of law in which Beatrice Wells repeatedly sues Jonathan Fontaine there are, from time to time, celebrity guests. Anita Hill has been known to show up, wearing her signature yellow suit and ancient, bookish hairstyle. Sometimes Strom Thurmond bursts in. "Hell hath no fury like a woman scorned!" the senator shouts, to no one in particular, his sad pate resting crookedly. He

269

might take a seat beside Anne Boleyn, cradling her own head in her lap, or Gloria Steinem in a flowing white wedding dress, signature blue glasses. They will abruptly stand and march out, as if this means something, but Beatrice is not sure what. She keeps her eyes steady on Jonathan Fontaine, looking for a twitch of regret.

"She overreacted," he's saying. "She clearly overreacted," he says.

It is hot inside the courtroom; somewhere "Thriller" plays, boys break dancing everywhere, whirling like tops all over Manhattan and Brooklyn and the Bronx, their knuckled spines spinning them so fast they're a blur against the asphalt, the sidewalks, the streets.

"She called the next day and rescinded her application," Jonathan Fontaine says. "Apoplectic, she sounded, quoting some dead suffragist, Sappho, Margaret Sanger, all of them." He turns to look at Beatrice Wells directly and raises a delicate finger. "You radical feminists need to get a sense of humor," he says. "You need to lighten up."

She would like to say something but in this version she has no voice; in this version her mouth opens and shuts like a fish unhooked from its line and tossed to shore.

"You don't know when to let up," he's saying. "You don't know when to let well enough alone. So I crossed the line a little bit. So I said it like it is, is that a crime?"

270

And here it's Frances Pearlman who steps in, her scratchy polyester pants announcing her. "It's a crime!" she roars.

"So sue me," Jonathan Fontaine says.

"She is!" Frances Pearlman roars. Beatrice recognizes the opened book Dr. Pearlman carries, its worn cover, its onionskin pages, the faint pencil marks of Pearlman's collected coven.

"You can't sue him," Beatrice Wells's mother says. They are on the telephone, Beatrice staring out to Grove Street, the wisteria twisting around the window, its vine arm thick, menacing as a snake. "If you sue him, it's all over."

"What do you mean?"

"You won't get any work. Ever. You'll be blackballed. You'll be labeled a troublemaker and you can just kiss everything else goodbye."

"It's illegal. I mean, he said it himself."

"That's a different thing."

"That's not a different thing. That's him admitting it; that's him knowing full well what he was doing. That's the thing. We make excuses; they come up with excuses. But they know full well and we let them get away with it. We make nice. Why isn't everyone furious? Why aren't we all just furious?"

"Who's we?" her mother says. "I'm not we. I'm me. And you're not we. You're you. Nobody's we; there's no we."

"Please, Mother."

"When I was your age it was a little more subtle: they asked our *method*," her mother says. "I remember one of the secretarial positions. They said, 'What *method* are you using?' And I had to laugh because I had no idea—I mean, if you'd said rhythm I would have thought castanets. I told you I didn't even sleep with your father until months after we were married."

Beatrice looks out the window at the brownstones across the way. "Yes," she says. "You told me," she says.

"Terrified, I was terrified. I'd hide in the bathroom. I mean, in those days nobody ever said a thing. Not one thing."

Beatrice counts to ten, remembering how, when she moved in, her mother there to help her, she'd waked the next morning to her mother sweeping the street, the entire length of Grove Street.

"So," her mother says. "Are you?"

"What?" Beatrice says.

"You know," her mother says. "Trying?"

In the other frequently played and truth be told unoriginal versions of their meeting, Beatrice Wells runs into Jonathan Fontaine in a restaurant (spits in his eye or maybe throws a drink), on a crowded bus (refuses his repeated requests to be acknowledged, stares him down cold), at a lecture celebrating the publication of a collection of her illustrations. (He waits in a long line to have her sign his book, attempting to apologize for the mistaken impression he must have given her—had he known she'd have such superhuman strength, such an extraordinary capacity for everything!) Now she wishes she had a bit more time, maybe a year or two more to get back on her feet. She would have liked to bump into Jonathan Fontaine at a gala or a museum, maybe at a busy restaurant while on a working lunch, someone else's dime, a player who stands when Jonathan Fontaine approaches—they've brokered many deals—and introduces her.

"Of course," Jonathan Fontaine says, sizing her up—her tailored, dark blue suit; her expensive hair. "Ms. Wells and I go way back," he says.

But fate has dealt her a different hand and here she is, quite suddenly, wandering among the outdoor holiday kiosks making small talk with Jonathan Fontaine, aged skates looped and hanging over her shoulder, hair crammed under a woolly winter hat. Yes, he's saying, he still lives in the East Seventies, and yes, he's saying, he's still at the office most mornings by 6:00 a.m. though no, he's saying, he no longer runs marathons, bad knees, creeping age, too much travel, the world smaller, compact, a summit every few weeks in farther-flung locations, a debilitating plane ride. This one will take him close to fifteen hours.

"And who will be there?" she asks, she can't help herself. "Who will be at the Future of Our World?"

"Oh, the usual suspects," Jonathan Fontaine says. His blue eyes water as he considers the scented candle she thought could make a nice presentation—its neutral beige matching any color scheme. "Fred and Ted. Bill and Will. Javier. Han and Dao. Andre. Oskar with a *k,*" he says. "Do you know them?"

"I haven't met them," she says.

Jonathan Fontaine shrugs. "Well, they'll be there," he says. "They're always there," he says.

"And women?" she asks. "Any mothers?"

She knows she's a total bore, transparent as glass, but somehow she can't help herself. She will ruin the party every time she opens her mouth but increasingly she can't help herself, remembering how she did not when she had the chance, sitting there, across from Jonathan Fontaine's wide desk in her small chair, remembering how she had said, No, how she had nodded and smiled, how she had walked to HR directly afterward to withdraw her application, how she had never called or read him any names from her Assembly book, how she had never invoked the wrath of Gloria, or Margaret, or Eleanor. At the very least, she might have quoted Eleanor. It seemed a shame to have never quoted Eleanor. On paper, this a small offense, perhaps—she wouldn't argue that—and yet water dripped for generations will drill a tunnel through solid rock. She knew in other places she might be wrapped in a tarp and sold for a dowry, held prisoner for the sins of her uncles, kept hidden under the draped folds of a heavy black blanket, traded into slavery, beaten regularly, drowned like a kitten at birth, and still, and still.

Jonathan Fontaine holds the scented, beige candle in his elegant fingers. He appears to be truly thinking, his hair blowing around; he appears to be racking his brain. "I don't know," he finally says, putting the candle back in its place. "Maybe Mary. Mary might be there, I think. Mary is sometimes there," he says.

The jury has reached its decision. The foreman in her smart pink jacket and gold brooch stands to read the verdict. First, though, she'd like to say a little something. If it please the court, she says, and the judge turns to her and Jonathan Fontaine stares at her and Beatrice Wells, in her place somewhere outside the imagining waits for her, and the lawyer, uncharacteristically, pauses for her; even the stenographer stops typing. The semibarren Anne Boleyn has returned, her head balanced on her shoulders; she leads Gloria Steinem in bunny ears and fishnet stockings, the lovely, ugly Eleanor, and the aged Girton girl, who carries a plate loaded with roast beef and roasted potatoes, creamed spinach. Frances Pearlman stumps down the aisle to a front seat, the scritch-scratch of her polyester pants unnerving.

"It all sucks," the foreman says.

"What?" says the judge.

"We're screwed," says the foreman. "Totally screwed."

"Twenty percent," says one of the women on the jury, the quiet one who has been embroidering throughout and seemed to barely give a damn. "Maybe thirty percent, thirty if we're lucky."

"Rarely thirty," another woman says; she is dark-skinned, older. "And what about women of color?"

"Sometimes thirty. In certain subjects, fifty, sixty, seventy—teaching, nursing," says a woman with large glasses.

"Ninety-three percent in prostitution," says the embroidering woman, biting off the thread.

"Tooth and nail, we get there. Crawling over hot coals," says the foreman. "There are sacrifices."

"There are always sacrifices," says the woman in the glasses.

"Sacrifices, hah!" says the judge. "I'm making less than this guy," she says, gesturing to the snoring man, who grunts and snaps his suspenders. "And my daughter? Jesus! She's in Hollywood!"

"It's not like none of us don't know," says the embroidering woman. "We all know."

"Not necessarily," says the youngest woman,

a pretty filly in her early twenties; she looks up from her handheld device and beams out at them. "To me you're speaking Greek."

"Did you hear that?" says the judge. "There's no we here. Only me. And I'm the judge. And I say, adjourned." She raises her gavel and is about to strike when from Frances Pearlman's chair comes what sounds like a steady mumbling, or humming, a noise that gets louder and louder as if, from the opened book in her lap, Frances Pearlman has let out a swarm of angry bees, though the rumble comes from Frances Pearlman herself, from the deep place within her, the diaphragm, where she has been taught to breathe in and breathe out, to emote, Frances Pearlman reading aloud, her glasses low on the bridge of her nose, her yellowy eyes fixed to the brittle pages, pausing only to lick her finger to turn the page, to continue.

The foreman watches for a moment then sits back down. The old man wakes, the jury listens, the judge pauses. An eerie quiet blankets all of them, the only sound the rising notes of Pearlman's recitation, the clicking consonants and vowels, the combinations of letters in a life lived, a woman born, the names pronounced then drifting down, lilting down, like snow, muffled by their own inconsequential accumulation, melting in the courtroom heat to be taken up as water, again, by the clouds.

It is the judge, from her high bench, who abruptly breaks the silence.

"Could somebody turn her off?" she says, banging her gavel hard.

In a kiosk called Shangri-la, amid wind chimes and handbags made from gum and candy wrappers, Beatrice Wells spots a cat-shaped trivet of molten glass, a functional art piece with a little tag attached telling the story of the trivet's creator and its proper washing instructions. "This is perfect," Jonathan Fontaine says. "You're a lifesaver," he says.

"Guilty," Beatrice Wells says. "They found you guilty."

"What?" Jonathan Fontaine says.

"What you said to me. About getting pregnant. That was against the law. It was none of your fucking business," she says. "You had no right to ask me. It didn't have a thing to do with anything. It had nothing to do with you."

"I don't remember," Jonathan Fontaine says.

"Oh yes you do," Beatrice says, as if she's reprimanding her boys. The sun has set behind the mecca of Times Square and now the streetlamps in Bryant Park switch on——magical. In front of her, Jonathan Fontaine smacks his hands together for warmth and reaches for the trivet. "This is perfect," he says. "You're a lifesaver," he says.

"Oh," Beatrice Wells says. "I'm happy to help."

He smiles at her then, his blue eyes softer, smooth as Ella's deep voice, beautiful as the exhausted girls with their American Girl dolls, sleeping in their mothers' laps in their taxis to their hotels, beautiful as her beautiful boys, suddenly huge, whooping and hollering in the dusky outline of the park, smacking someone's jacket against one of the sycamore limbs, a wedged Ping-Pong ball, a particularly forceful serve. "How old?" Jonathan Fontaine says.

"Charlie's fifteen," she says. "Sam's ten."

"A handful," he says.

"You can say that again," she says.

She watches as Jonathan Fontaine grips his trivet, his raw hands rough, the scratch from her skate blade almost completely disappeared, a thin white line. "This is perfect," he says. "You're a lifesaver."

"It was the principle of the thing," she says. "Sure, I could have lied. I could have not given a damn. But it wasn't fair. It isn't fair."

"Well," Jonathan Fontaine says. "Best of luck with them. Best of luck with everything."

"Great to see you," Beatrice Wells says. "It was really great to see you," she says. They have walked away from the kiosks and stand on one of the steps leading back down to Forty-second Street, Beatrice shivering a bit, thinking she might suggest to the boys that they get their hot chocolates before skating, that they maybe bag the whole thing given how the day's turned cold, how the boys have worked up such a froth on the Ping-Pong table—they weren't even into it, anyway. She had cajoled them here, she knew, saying how it had been forever since they'd had an outing like this, telling them how she'd recently found her old skates. She hadn't worn them since high school, she'd said. Come on, come on, she'd said. Please? "This is perfect," Jonathan Fontaine says. "You're a lifesaver."

"And you're a son of a bitch," Beatrice Wells says. "Charlie! Sam!"

"Goodbye," Jonathan Fontaine says. "Thank you, again." He moves in to kiss Beatrice and she, somewhat startled, tilts her face toward his, closing her eyes, smelling the cold of his scarf, his face, lingering. "My pleasure," she says into the soft wool. "Goodbye," she says, holding on though he's already gone, disappearing as quickly into the crowd as he'd suddenly appeared out of it—a random encounter, an accident of timing.

"Are we going?" Charlie says. He's run over, panting. "Sam's toast."

"He cheated," Sam says, catching up. "He like totally cheated."

"Loser," Charlie says.

"He totally cheated, Mom. I'm telling you the truth," Sam says.

Her boys' flushed faces look as ravenous to her as they did when they were little, smaller boys, when sometimes, after a particularly exuberant snowfall, on a snow day, they would all three take the subway to Columbus Circle and walk into Central Park, their sleds the cafeteria trays she insisted were just as good as anything you could buy. Then the boys wouldn't let her out of their sight; then they'd make a train and slide down, the ice and the snow and the wind stinging her cheeks as she shut her eyes and felt the world drop away.

"Come on," she says to them now. "I want to show you something."

Beatrice Wells has been skating with her boys for what feels like hours, long after most of the tourists have gone to their various preshow dinners, long after children are in bed, businessmen and businesswomen at home, offices shuttered, stores closed, restaurants filled, the subway rumbling underground, relentlessly crisscrossing the city, east to west, north to south. In Queens, in the yellow, sickly light of a JFK terminal, Jonathan Fontaine will soon board a direct flight for Beijing and, despite two Ambien and several glasses of good wine, have trouble sleeping, the flesh wound throbbing, worsening throughout the long trip until, in Beijing, he will seek out Mary at the first gathering. She will say, in no uncertain terms, that he needs medical attention. Pronto, she will say. But for now, he remains unaware.

For now, he sits in the JFK executive lounge, in the seat that he has always liked best, near the big plate-glass windows where he can watch the planes taking off, landing, the drama of their lights in the dusk, the blinking red warnings, the blurry yellows, the stark whites.

He thinks of Beatrice Wells every now and again, or rather his mind drifts that way, to her face, still pretty underneath that ridiculous hat, to her strapping boys. Boys who now hold hands, their mother's hand linked back to them, the last in line or maybe, from a different angle, the first. This is exactly what she wants, she has told them: she wants them to go fast, as fast as they can, and they promise they will, and they do, and when they are not quite enough they enlist all the others—the guy in the fur vest, a few lingering instructors, a couple from Australia, young backpackers staying at the YMCA—the all of them forming the whip, circling around and around and around on the thin ice of the artificial pond, building a mounting speed as Beatrice holds tight, almost ready to let go. At any moment, she thinks, eyes pressed shut, she will let go; at any moment, she thinks. Any moment.

Acknowledgments

My great thanks to the editors of the publications that first published many of these stories, as well as to Sarah Gorham, who took a chance on *Where She Went*, and Nan Graham, who continues to take chances on everything.

Enormous gratitude to Rafael, Delia, and Iris, for every moment, and to my mother, for her love of a good story.

CREDITS

These stories originally appeared, sometimes in different form, in the following publications: "M&M World" and "Playdate" in *The New Yorker*; "Conversation" and "Slow the Heart," in *The Yale Review*; "The Blue Hour," in *The Paris Review*; "Do Something" in *Ploughshares*; "Radical Feminists," in *A Public Space*; "Paris, 1994," in *Press*.

"The Blue Hour" and "Paris, 1994" were previously published in *Where She Went* (Sarabande Books, 1996). "Playdate," "Conversation," and "Do Something" were previously published in *A Short History of Women* (Scribner, 2009).

"M&M World" and "Do Something" were selected for *The Best American Short Stories*, 2012, 2007.

ABOUT THE AUTHOR

Kate Walbert is the author of six previous books of fiction, including *His Favorites*; *The Sunken Cathedral*, named a best book of the year by the *San Francisco Chronicle*; *A Short History of Women*, one of the *New York Times Book Review*'s ten best books of the year and a finalist for the Los Angeles Times Book Prize; and *Our Kind*, a National Book Award finalist.

She is a recipient of a Dorothy and Lewis B. Cullman Fellowship at the New York Public Library, a National Endowment for the Arts Fellowship in Fiction, and a Connecticut Commission for the Arts Fellowship. Her work has appeared in *The New Yorker*, *The Paris Review*, *The Best American Short Stories*, and *The O. Henry Prize Stories*. She lives in New York with her family.

Center Point Large Print
600 Brooks Road / PO Box 1
Thorndike, ME 04986-0001 USA

(207) 568-3717

US & Canada:
1 800 929-9108
www.centerpointlargeprint.com